THE SUN STAR

was a weak red giant that kept the
planet's northern sky ruddy with
half-light. The tangled mass of the
Halcyon Drift lurked higher, crouching behind the red haze like a vast
crippled spider suspended on a tenuous web of starlight.

*Technically the Drift was a dark nebula.
Even at high noon, it had an angry, sullen
glow which rivaled the weak sunlight. The
perennial ebb and flow of its contortive currents made it hard to look at for long—the
star-storms were always blasting matter back
and forth in time, and from its light-dense
core to its thin shell.*

*"It looks terrible," Even said. "Like a great
hand with crippled fingers that keep clutching
and coiling."*

*"That's what it feels like too," I told her.
"Fingers always plucking at your skin, poking into your shields. It fumbles spaceships
to pieces like a child pulling apart a fly."*

**Nevertheless, their goal lay at the
core of that cosmic hurricane.**

Brian M. Stableford

THE
HALCYON
DRIFT

DAW BOOKS, INC.
DONALD A. WOLLHEIM, PUBLISHER

1301 Avenue of the Americas
New York, N. Y.   10019

Dedication:

For Val and Maureen

FIRST PRINTING, 1972

PRINTED IN U.S.A.

THE
HALCYON
DRIFT

Prologue

───────

It is on a world whose name I do not know, on the slopes of a great mountain, that the *Javelin* came down. She is surrounded by black boulders which are too heavy for a man to move. I have sealed the cracks in her silver skin with mud and clay, but she no longer has a door. Inside, she is not badly damaged—the drive chamber and the tailfins are shattered beyond all hope, but the living quarters are still sound. If it were not for the fact that she was built to stand upright, but lies on her side, she would be comfortable. But who can sleep in a vertical bunk?

Some thirty or forty yards from the ship there is a cross planted in the ground. It marks Lapthorn's grave. It is a shallow grave, because there is not a great deal of dirt caught in the crack between the faces of implacable rock. The cross is often blown down, as though the wind is able to seek it out and pluck it away. Lapthorn is not welcome here; neither am I. The wind continually tells me so.

To right and left, as I look down the mountain, the view is excised by more gigantic slopes of languid black rock, but before my resting place is a channel which leads down to the plain and away across the ashen desert. Far off, beyond the expended sands, more mountains form a distant wall which shines all colors from red to violet as the sun walks the gray sky from dawn till dusk. Brown clouds move sullenly across the sulky face of the sky, washing the black mountain faces with hazy tears. The sparse bushes, the shifting sand, the gray ridges are obscured by a constant floating dust which likewise changes color with the advancing hours of every day.

I wear a long beard. My hair is never cut save for the tufts which threaten to invade my eyes and rob me of sight. I take no pride in cleanliness. I live in misery and regret, and make no effort to assert my humanity. I am an invader, a beast. There is no need to remind myself that I belong elsewhere. I am not wanted here.

Another day is draining away, and the desert is cold tedious blue-turning-gray. I was not always so despairing. I used to go down every evening to the plain to bring water from the small pools which are constantly maintained by the rain which flows from the slopes. I would bring water for washing as well as for drinking. But I found that I could carry water enough for three days if I did not bother to wash, and I grew idle, long ago. I used to occupy my days in mending my ill-used home, in trying to improve the meager quality of my life here. I mounted expeditions to all points of the compass, and planned even longer ones. I scaled the mountain and considered the circumnavigation of the world which I had inherited by virtue of being stranded. But what I found on the peak, in the far plain, and on other slopes never repaid the effort I put into reaching them, and mental fatigue soon drowned my adventure with pointlessness.

The present never occupies my mind. Every day is identical, and there is no use in counting them, nor profit in trying to make each one individual in any way. When my mind wanders, it is never to tomorrow or yesterday, but always deep into the past—before the *Javelin* lifted from some inconsequental rim world on the journey which would result in her death, and Lapthorn's death, and my despair. I remember other worlds, other times, other ships.

I once lived a while on the darkside of a world which circled close to a blue giant sun. The ships had to creep in and out of ports hidden in deep caves, fully shielded against the fearsome torrent of radiation. There was no habitable place in the system save for the deep, labyrinthine ways of the inner world. The people lived in cities built in the planet's honeycomb heart, away from the lethal light and the cold of darkness. The air was always hot and loaded with odors—a background stench of faint decay and sweat, and heavy perfume intended to drown and disguise it, since it could not be concealed. The most valued thing on the planet was light—sof light, kind light, warming light, soothing light, painless light. All worlds want most what they cannot find around them. With a brightside that was an inferno, and a darkside that could see no stars, this planet bred people who knew the true beauty and presence of light, who could savor its texture and understand the inner qualities of its makeup. Lapthorn and I used to take our ship—it was the old *Fire-Eater* then— back and forth in search of all manner of lighting devices —exotic lamps and equally exotic substances to fuel them.

After three years of trading with the world and living there fifty days in every hundred, Lapthorn swore that he could tell the color of light with the follicles of his skin, and taste its texture with his tongue. He was beginning to babble about the search for the perfect light when I thought it was time to move on to fresh pastures. Lapthorn was like that—impressionable, sensitive. Every world left something in his character. I'm different. I'm a realist.

Another time we worked, for a while, for the great library at New Alexandria. Lapthorn didn't like that, because it was in the inner wheel—the great highway of star civilization. Earth was too far out from the rich worlds to remain the hub of human existence. New Alexandria, New Rome, New Israel, and Penaflor were our homes in the stars. They were our new heritage, the focus of our future. Lapthorn hated them, and craved the distant shores. He loved the feel of alien soil, the heat of alien suns, the love of alien women. But there was better money, come by far more easily, in the core, and we needed to scrap the *Fire-Eater* before she fire-ate herself and us with her. Hence the New Alexandria job.

We spent the best part of two years tracking down alien knowledge and literature commissioned by the library. The books we found were in a thousand languages, many of which were completely unknown save to the people who wrote them down. But the problems of translation weren't any of our concern. We just located the books, procured them by fair means or foul, and carted them to the library. I liked that job, and even Lapthorn admitted that it was good in parts—the parts we spent on the alien worlds.

Oddly enough, I think that was the most dangerous job I ever did. I found that aliens (pretty much like humans, I suppose) are perfectly logical where major matters like money are concerned, but absurdly touchy about certain trivial objects no good to man or beast.

The sky is as black as the mountains now. The desert plain is invisible. I light the fire. The light hasn't much warmth. Lapthorn would have complained of its dull color and its foul taste. But it's all I have. The ship retains a reservoir of power, but all of it is directed to one single purpose—maintaining the faint, surely futile, mayday bleep which is my solitary hope of eventual rescue. The bleep has a limited range, and no ship is likely to pass within it, because I am within the fringes of a dark nebula, where no sane captain would bring his ship. But the bleep is my one link with the universe beyond the mountain, and it surely deserves every last vestige of the *Javelin's* power.

Agitated by the wind, clouds of sand rustle against the lower slopes. The fire crackles. The wind seems to be deliberately shifting so that wherever I sit it can blow smoke into my eyes. It's a malicious wind this one. Lapthorn's cross will be down again in the morning. Moths attracted by the fire, flit back and forth above the flames, casting shadow-flickers in the light reflected from the smoke column.

The sparks that fly away from the fire remind me of stars. I wish that I were a moth, to fly away from this little world, among the stars again. The wind knows about this idle dream, and uses it to taunt me. It whispers in my ears. It's the wind which brings back all these memories of other worlds, other times—indirectly, at least, by driving me to avoid its presence and insistence.

After New Alexandria, when we had our beautiful new ship, I let Lapthorn have his head for a while. We went out to the rim and wandered, searching new worlds for new ways to make money. There was little or no profit to be made, little or no comfort to be had, and we did no good for ourselves. Lapthorn fell in love at least twice, but it never lasted long with Lapthorn, whether it was a woman or a world. Events left their scars and their souvenirs, but nothing monopolized Lapthorn's soul for more than a short space of time.

We traded with the Lakshmi, whose adults look like gold-winged flies, and whose children grow in the ground like trees from eggs like knotty roots. Males exist only in the vegetative phase. One generation of adults pollinate the female flowers of the next, and the pistils of the flowers serve as pupae carrying already-gravid female flies. Even Lapthorn found little in this race to touch his heart, although for a while he showed a tendency to talk to trees, and once or twice I saw him looking at fireflies with a delighted air of mystery in his expression.

We lived with the dog-faced Magliana, in villages strung between the treetops in a webwork of branches and creepers, far above a vast equatorial swamp covering half a world.

Lapthorn was bitten by a snake on Varvarin, and would have died of it but for the nomads of the district, who saved his life in return for one of his hands. They took the hand and dissolved the flesh away. They reconnected the bones with copper wire and one of them wore it around his neck as a pendant. Few of the nomads had two hands, and almost all of them wore one or more displayed in some prominent fashion on his person. A hand worn around the neck or at the waist will never strangle you or steal from you. This is especially relevant if you have enemies. The nomads had. But they were healers and they healed Lapthorn. Help always has a price, and some are strange. I contrived to keep both of my hands on my arms. I had to. A one-handed engineer can still do his job, but a one-handed pilot is worthless.

On Bira, we both got hooked on the nectar of the scorpion lilies, which grew only in the dawn, and faded once the sun was clear of the horizon. But the local day was two standard years long, and the dawn lingered long. We followed sunrise around the planet for half a year, until we reached the shore of an uncrossable sea. There would be no more lilies until the dawn reached the far shore. Hundreds of the natives had taken the same ecstatic trek, and over half of them died in the throes of withdrawal. Those who did not began the return journey, to wait for the sun again. They were a slender, sickly people, but Lapthorn and I had stronger stomachs and stronger minds.

We returned only so far as our ship, and left for a different shore.

Not even Lapthorn really got what he wanted out of those years on the fringe. His craving for new ideas and new experiences was never satiated. He seemed to have an infinite capacity for change. Everything added a new facet to his personality. He was never full up, never exhausted. I think Lapthorn might have found the secret of eternal youth. He was still healthy and strong when he died coaxing the drive of the *Javelin*, while I remained unhurt at the controls. When a ship goes down, it is usually the pilot's fault, but the engineer invariably suffers most.

In the meantime, nothing made any impression on me. Maybe I had the secret of eternal age. The star-worlds had nothing to teach me. They had not the capacity to change me. Lapthorn said that I had no soul. I suppose that we were competely mismatched. In fact, our partnership never really contained any harmony. We worked together simply because we had started out together, and neither of us could afford to break away. I suppose Lapthorn was enough of a dreamer not to care too much about who was up front, because all that mattered to him was where we were going and where we'd already been. And I didn't give a damn who was down below as long as his drive unit never let me down.

But all we collected in years of fringe-running was a reputation. The cargoes we carried never made a fortune, but they created rumors. The stories we could tell about ourselves were impressive, and contained enough truth for later voyagers to confirm that we might actually have done what we said. Lapthorn liked people to talk about us.

The fire is dying. It's time for sleep. I wish that for once I didn't have to go to bed hungry. But I wish the same things every night. There's not much that's edible growing on the mountain or living down in the desert. The ship's supplies of deep-space gruel ran out some time ago. Somehow, though, I don't starve. I chew leaves and I snare mice, and I contrive to live. But I'm always hungry. Perhaps I ought to be thankful that I haven't poisoned myself. But the world sustains my kind of life. Just. I'm not wanted, but I'm tolerated, because I'm not too much of a nuisance. The world might not have liked Lapthorn though. And there's the wind, of course, which wants someone to talk to, a memory to stir, a mind to invade.

I don't think that I'm going mad. Loneliness is supposed to send men mad, and any other man would begin to get worried when the wind talked to him. But not me. Lapthorn said I have no soul. I can't go mad. I'm a realist. I'm stuck with myself, with my sanity. I hear the wind speak, therefore the wind speaks. No argument, no worry. I don't talk back. I listen, but I don't react. Nothing this world can do to me will elicit any response. I don't give in to alien worlds. I give way only to myself. Nothing reaches me from out there.

After the fringe, I tried to come back into the really big markets, in search of a killing. Guns, cosmetics, jewelry, and drugs were all hot markets, with constant demand and irregular supply. Anything in which fashion rules instead of utility is a good market for the trader—and that includes weaponry as well as decoration and edification. I reckoned that we had the initiative to dig out the best, and I was right, but times had moved on while we were out on the rim with the dropouts, and we failed at the other end—the outlets. We couldn't get a fair price, with the middlemen moving into the star-worlds in droves, quoting the Laws of New Rome, and the ordinances of wherever they happened to be, and never moving their hands from their gun butts. It was enough to sour anyone against life in the inner circle. I began to sympathize with Lapthorn's dislike of the human way of life.

We stuck with it for a while, because I thought Lapthorn's genius for digging out the best gems and the most exciting drugs might see us through. But it was useless. The little people seemed to take an excessive delight in cheating us and leaning on us because we were known. The other free traders talked about us. We were the best, by their lights. But we weren't system-beaters. We weren't equipped for dealing with that kind of problem. We had no alternative but to return to small trading, alien to alien. Lapthorn wasn't sorry, of course, and my sorrow was more for the evil ways of the world in general than for our own small part in the human condition.

We settled down, eventually, in the other rim, helping to push it even further out. Right back at the beginning, the

rim had been a burden I'd borne for Lapthorn's sake, and
civilization a burden he'd borne for mine. We'd taken
turns to call the tune, each of us chafing under the other's
yoke, building up the resentment and the determination
to flip the coin back over again. But in the end, we stopped
fighting and drifted.

I suppose neither of us was ever happy. Lapthorn's
dreams were impossible—there was never any conclusion
to which he could follow them. He followed them further
with me than he could have with anyone else, but I still
couldn't find him a destination. And in the meantime, I
wouldn't have been happy anywhere or anyhow. I'm just
not a happy man. Lapthorn said that I have no soul.

A lot of spacemen are like me. Cold, emotionless men
who don't inherit any part of the worlds and the people
that they see. There are a few fake Lapthorns—with his
vulnerability but without his inexhaustibility—but eventually they always go native somewhere. If they can be
reached, they're taken. If not by one world, then by the
next. Only Lapthorn lasted almost forever. Most of the
men who live long enough among the stars to crash on
some ridiculous, forlorn world like this one are my type
of spaceman—the maverick kind, the lone wolves, the men
with hearts of stone, the men without souls.

I sleep in the control room, because my bunk is wrong
way up, and the control room is the only space big enough
for the wall to make an adequate floor and vice versa. The
old *Fire-Eater* wasn't quite so cramped, for all that the
Javelin was a better ship. And was she, though? The *Fire-
Eater* never went down.

Even in here, the voice of the wind can reach me. There
isn't any door to keep it out, but even if there were, the
voice would find a way. I have difficulty getting to sleep,
but it isn't wholly the fault of the wind. It's the hunger
and the timelessness. I'd sleep all the time if I could, but
I'm saturated far too easily, and sleep is never easy to find
if you're already brimful of it.

When I drift away from consciousness, in search of
elusive sleep, I think about people.

There was Herault, back on Earth, before Lapthorn and
I sealed our unlikely alliance and bought the *Fire-Eater*
with our pooled funds. I was very young then, and Herault

was old. He must be dead by now. It was seven years since I'd last been home to see him. Lapthorn had relented once or twice before that and let me make a landfall on home, but he hated Earth like poison, and I'd let him divorce me from the planet as well, eventually. But even Lapthorn had liked Herault. He'd been a good man to work for and he'd taught me a great deal about spaceships and spacemen. I learned to fly the *Fire-Eater* by feel —to use her sensor web as if it were my own eyes and my own body—but it was Herault who talked me into that feel, who knew how to acquire it and make sure that I did. They don't fly like that these days, because they don't think it's necessary. The flying schools teach them to trust their machines, not to become a part of them. It works— in clear space, on planned runs. But not in the outer rim, and out in the galactic center. That's why civilization is the inner rim, and not the heart itself.

Herault taught Lapthorn the drive as well. A dimension-skipper is supposed to be easy to handle, but Herault didn't let Lapthorn think he could get away without knowing everything there was to know. If it hadn't been for Herault, we'd never have got into space. If it hadn't been for Herault, we'd never have lasted as long as we had. We'd never even have made it to this forsaken rock on the rim of nowhere. I'm grateful to Herault for all he did and tried to do. I'm sorry it ended up like this, and so would Herault be, if he knew.

More people.

On Peniel there was a girl called Myane. On Rocholt there was Dorcas, on Alhagayel there was Joan, on Doreniken there was Ophinia. Not an impressive list. Not a meaningful list anymore. There were no others worth remembering, and even these are not the most cherished memories. I could forget them without difficulty. Lapthorn could have remembered half a hundred, the smell and the taste of every one. He could have gorged himself on the delicacies of his remembrance. But they just didn't matter enough to me.

Alachakh was my friend. He was a Khormon trader. I saved his life once, on Veneto. He saved Lapthorn's, on Beckhofen. Lapthorn saved mine, on San Calogero. I'm not sure that things happened in that order. We were around together a lot, Alachakh and I. Not because we flew together, or because we chased each other's cargoes, but because we thought the same way. Alachakh and his engineer—Cuvio—were a counterpart to Lapthorn and myself. His ship—the *Hymnia*—was a sleek Khormon craft. I bought the *Javelin* because she was the closest human ship to the *Hymnia*. Alachakh is one of the few men I've every liked, and one of the few men Lapthorn held in high regard. Even the mavericks need to talk to each other, once now and again. Even the mavericks need to like somebody, to have somebody that they'd make an effort for, to have someone they could rely on for help.

I'm awake again now, and I shouldn't be. It's still dark and I have no right to be waking up in the middle of the night. Did something wake me? Perhaps it was Lapthorn's cross falling over again. The wind is here and it's plucking at my face, running chilly fingers across my eyes. I won't listen to it. I only want to go back to sleep.

—You've got to listen, it's saying. I can reach you and you know it. I can touch you whenever I want. I'm all the way inside of you.

It's not true. Nothing ever reaches me. There's no alien world, no alien being, no alien feeling, can leave a mark in my mind.

—I can.

Did I really hear something? Shall I get up and look around? Maybe it's an animal or an insect. Was, I mean. It's gone now.

—I'm not gone, says the whispering wind. I'm with you now. I knew you'd have to let me in, and you have. I'm not wind anymore, I'm a voice in your head. I'm all here. You can't get away from me now, not even if you *do* run back to the stars. I'm part of you now, all wrapped up in your mind. You can't ever be free of me.

I'm going back to sleep.

People.

Benwyn, Quivira, Emerich, Rothgar. Rothgar, now—it's worth thinking about Rothgar for a while. An easy man to remember. Thought he was a great big man inside his thin frame. Hard drinker. Meant trouble for most of the ships which took him on because few of their captains could handle him and even fewer could stand to have him around. He knew all the engines and must have worked them on well over a hundred ships—big liners, p-shifters, ramrods, even Khormon dredgers and Gallacellan ships. He was a genius in his way. But what's the point of genius if you haven't the temperament to apply it? He was the best man to have underneath you that any pilot could find. He put the power where it was needed, gave you thrust when you asked for it, made the drive do the impossible to get you through a tough spot. But he was condemned nevertheless to spending half his life bumming around spaceports touting for work. But he was his own man, though. Nobody owned Rothgar, except for a little bit at a time. Nobody could scare him. Nobody could make him do anything he didn't want to do. Rothgar was the most unyielding man I ever knew.

Places.

A million of them. Little bits of big words. Single moments of odd places. One day later in choosing a path through the galaxy, one day later in setting down on each world, and I'd see the whole lot differently. They'd be different moments, different little bits of the same worlds. Nobody ever gets to *know* the star-worlds, no matter how much you absorb. They touch you, but only with the tips of your fingers. You deal in tiny fragments, not in whole entities. They touched me lightest of all. I have memories, but they're faded, like old photographs. Unreal, Lapthorn's memories would be as bright as white stars—he'd be forever taking them out and polishing them up, in case he needed one in a hurry. Every one would be a jewel—a living light. What must it have been to be Lapthorn? To see so clearly, feel so deeply.

Was it, I wonder, a tragedy that I lived and Lapthorn died? Should the ship have come down headfirst instead of belly-flopped? Would the broken drive have killed him anyway? Was it my fault that Lapthorn died? Could I have crashed in such a fashion that Lapthorn lived, even if it meant that I died? Should I have, if I could?

But Lapthorn must have died here anyway, in time. He would have drained away, into its drabness and its perpetual misery. He *needed* the stimulation of the worlds whose selves he tried to absorb into his own. He needed light of a special kind, did Lapthorn. To him, this world would have become a limitless darkness in a very short time. Maybe it will get me that way too—bore me to death, kill me with a dismal everpresence.

It's the wind again.

Please go away and let me sleep. It's so insistent tonight, as though it had a point to make. Perhaps it *is* getting through to me after all. Perhaps it has invaded my mind. No man can withstand pressure forever. Maybe even I give in, in the end.

—It's not a matter of giving in. I'm with you, but I'm real. It's the real world that we're in.

Maybe so, my friend, I reply. Perhaps, now that you're here, I should just accept the fact. But you've not treated me kindly.

—I had to find a way in, the wind replied. It's never easy.

Sometimes I'll swear it understands every thought I think. A clever wind, this. An educated one. Needing my attention, like a little child. But why? Why do you want to be a part of *me*? Why do you want to live in *my* mind?

—I need you. I need somewhere to *be*. I need someone to hold me. I need a host.

You're marooned here as well, I suppose.

—Yes.

How come?

—Others died here.

Not humans. This world's unmarked on my charts. Undiscovered, unvisited. We're right on the edge of the Halcyon Drift. A bad place. It must have been the Drift that brought us down. It was either radiation or distortion, and there's plenty of both in the Drift. But no human ship has ever tried to map the Drift. If you came here in a ship, it was an alien.

—It was an alien, the wind confesses.

I realize finally that I'm not alone, that the voice belongs to another sentient being. It's not the wind at all—not really. It's an alien mind parasite, and I'm its new host. I don't know whether to be glad or sad.

I thought you didn't want me here. I thought you kept blowing down the cross on Lapthorn's grave.

—I had to get inside you, the wind explains. I had to make you take notice.

And what are you, now you're inside me? Are you the soul that Lapthorn said I hadn't got? Are you the voice of my conscience? What are you, alien wind? What are you made of?

—I'm made of you. I am you. But I won't bother you. Talk to you, perhaps—help you, if I can. But I'm not going to cause you any trouble.

In case I throw you out?

—You can't throw me out. In case you become an unsuitable host. I have to live with you now, and you with me.

It's going on for morning now. The sun is coming up. For all my lack of sleep, I don't feel tired. I think I'll get up and go outside.

I feel better than I've felt for some time, and I'm not sure why. Oddly enough, it isn't because the wind throws up a wall between myself and loneliness. To tell the truth, I don't care much either way about the wind. Maybe it will bother me, maybe it won't. But it's here now and there's nothing I can do about it. But I don't *need* the wind. I'm not Lapthorn. I'm adequate enough, all by myself.

It's a bright red morning. The sun sparkles shyly. Silver sky instead of gray. But the black slopes are just as dismal. Nothing changes them. There are little wisps of cloud wandering from east to west. And something shining, like a little star, is coming toward me.

It's a ship.

I know now what wakened me in the night. It was the ship going over, trying to get a fix on my bleep. And now they have it, and they're coming down in the plain. I'm free.

—I'm going with you. For life.

I don't care. I'm going home.

I'll just go and stand up the cross that marks Lapthorn's grave.

I

The ship that picked me up was a ramrod, the *Ella Marita,* owned by the Caradoc Company and skippered by a Penaflor Eurasian named Axel Cyran. I dare say that if you were to encounter Cyran in a good mood he would strike you as a reasonably ordinary, fairly decent kind of spaceman. I never got a chance to see his good side. Working for a cutthroat gang like Caradoc can ruin anybody.

The Caradoc Company is one of a hundred or more trading combines with minor spacefleets, each one trying to organize, stabilize, and monopolize some tiny fraction of the galaxy's trade. At this time, flow from the rim to the innner wheel was building up into a flood and everyone with money wanted to ride in on the tide of prosperity. The hub worlds—particularly Penaflor, Valerius, and New Alexandria—were interested in reliability and results. Like everybody else, Caradoc was trying to make a big name for itself. Many things stood in its way. One of them was the free traders—the thousand or so little ships which knew the ground, had made the contacts, and stubbornly refused to cooperate with the companies. Ergo, Caradoc didn't like free traders. Most especially, they didn't like the men from whom the free traders claimed to take their lead—the ones they talk most about. Including me.

Cyran wasn't pleased to see me. He seemed to think that I'd got in his way. He called me a bloody pirate and told me I'd wasted good company money luring his ship from its assigned mission to pick me up. I began to wonder exactly why he *had* picked me up, and I was half afraid he might throw me back.

I expressed my sincere gratitude to the captain, and even apologized for putting him to so much bother. I refrained from asking any questions which he might see as impertinent—like what the hell was he doing in the Halcyon Drift anyway? I remained extremely unpopular. In the end, I decided I'd be better off talking to nobody, just sticking to my bunk and accepting the gruel they handed out with all the gratitude I could feign. The crew looked after me as well as they could, but Cyran really had it in for me and he was always on their necks. I could see that the captain had obviously had a very worrying time inside the Drift—who wouldn't?—but I couldn't really excuse his conduct on that basis. I'd have paid him gladly for all his trouble, but I hadn't a sou. The stuff that I'd crammed into my packsack before going to meet the *Ella Marita* was all junk, and mostly Lapthorn's junk at that—souvenirs and keepsakes. Even Lapthorn hadn't anything of value— you can't cart a curio collection around in a starship—and what there was wouldn't raise the price of a shirt in any port in the galaxy.

I had plans to duck ship and fade away as soon as we touched the tarpol in the landing bay, wherever we were, but it didn't work out that way. The ramrod's base was Hallsthammer, and it was close enough for Cyran to be still seething when we set down. He still wanted a scapegoat for his bad trip and I was it. He had me arrested and transferred me to the p-shifter which the Caradoc fleet used for liaison with home base on Earth.

The p-shifter took me to New Rome, and the Caradoc lawyers hauled me into court with a claim for compensation as a result of the *Ella Marita*'s detour to salvage me. News of my pickup must have traveled very fast, because I was a joke on New Rome practically before I touched down there. The idea of a salvage claim against a spaceman seemed funny to them. It wasn't nearly so funny to me, especially when I had to watch the case go against me every inch of the way. The Law of New Rome sticks anywhere in the galaxy, no matter what the local law might be. In order to stick like that it has to be dependable and enforceable, and above all fair. The New Romans made no claim that their system had anything to do with *justice* —it was law and law only. But for the most part it protected the like of *us* from the likes of *them*. The *Ella Marita* salvage case, however, was a clear-cut victory for *them*. A charge of twenty thousand was placed on the rescue, and an award made against any pay I might accumulate. I might have been flattered—nobody had ever suggested to me that my hide was worth anywhere near that amount—but for the first few days I was too sick. In addition, the Caradoc Company took out insurance against the recovery of their money and charged the premiums to me. Which meant that if I were lucky enough to live to be a hundred, Caradoc and the insurance company would divide every penny I made between them, and even if I died next week, Caradoc wouldn't lose unless they murdered me.

All this did not add up to a nice prospect. But at least while the p-shifter was on New Rome I got a little medical attention, and began to get back into some sort of reasonable shape. Alachakh heard I'd been picked up, and sent me a message of congratulation. Obviously he didn't know about the legal tangle. News travels slowly on the rim.

In the end, out of the kindness of their hearts, the Caradoc men let me ride on the p-shifter when it went back to Earth. All free, gratis and for nothing—a gesture of pure goodwill. One has to be grateful for small mercies.

It might have been more sensible to wait until I could hitch a lift to Penaflor, where the commercial spacelines were mostly based, and where the major shipyards were. But hitching rides on spaceships isn't easy, and I'd have had to live on charity while I was on New Rome. At least Caradoc was willing to feed me gruel in return for their blood money. Besides which, I was so damned tired I only wanted to run home and hide. Earth was all the home I had. Maybe nobody there knew me, except old Herault, but it was where I'd started out from. It was where I was born (at least, I presume so—no reliable account of the incident survives, and it's possible I was dumped there at an early age).

In any case, I ended up back in New York spaceport. I had enough loose change in my pockets for a couple of meals and a bus ride into the city, and that was about all.

Not that there was much point in going to New York City proper—the port was practically a city in its own right, and if work was to be found, it would be here.

Bearing in mind that even a condemned man was entitled to a hearty meal, I found a cheap hole on the north side of the port connurbation and rediscovered the delights of imitation food. It was my first almost-honest meal in two years, give or take a month, and recon or not it tasted beautiful compared to deep-space gruel and alien grass.

After I'd invested time in pampering my stomach, I sat back to relax and indulge in a little harmless self-pity.

That opened the door.

—It's no good crying about it.

I explained that I wasn't crying. I am in no way a slave to my emotions. I told the wind that I was merely regretting the more unfortunate aspects of the situation, and thinking that things could be better.

—You're a sham, Grainger, said the wind. You're no man of steel. You feel, just like everybody else. You're just ashamed to admit it.

The wind hadn't been around too long then, so it still made mistakes. It had made itself comfortable in my mind, but it hadn't quite got acclimatized yet. It still didn't know me, let alone understand me.

Let me alone, I requested. End of argument. I decided at that time to think of it as "he" thereafter. It was not that either his voice or his manner was in any way masculine, it was simply that to call it "she" would have introduced sexual overtones to the presence that were completely unwarranted. The wind hadn't told me anything about itself beyond the fact that it had been cast away on the Halcyon rock just as I had. I knew nothing about his nature or his history—only that he was with me for life and that he seemed to have every intention of treating his new home with the respect which any good home deserves. I'm told that children often talk to nonexistent companions, but that they grow out of it. I sometimes wonder whether they just don't grow out of telling other people about their companions.

It was late at night—going on for midnight—and the owner threw me out before I'd really had my fill of sitting in his chair. Once precipitated from the warmth, I was also hurled right back into my problem. Where could I go and what did I do?

I had to go looking for Herault. There was no one else I might look for on the whole planet, and certainly no one else in the New York environs. It was the obvious place to go—the only chance, really. But I was reluctant, because I knew there was probably no Herault to be found. Ageless and indestructible, he'd seemed, when I'd last seen him— seven years ago. But he'd been old. Under Earth conditions—particularly New York conditions—it's rare in this day and age for a man to reach sixty, and Herault must have been past that ten years ago. The poisons of Earth accumulate in all of its children, no matter how strong or indomitable they might be. And the mental stress of living beyond our understanding puts a strain on all of our hearts. Herault might have been working still even on the last day of his life. But he couldn't live forever.

I didn't want to go knocking on Herault's door to be answered by a stranger, who didn't give a damn whether Herault was dead or not, to be told that no one of that name lived there. But what else could I do?

I was ten miles from Herault's place, and I'd already walked three or four from the spacefield. But I dragged my feet along in the right direction somehow. I wasn't in the best of health after two years on Lapthorn's Grave (I named the world on the spur of the moment), and that was a long ten miles. It took me over three hours, and by the time I arrived I was frozen stiff and dead tired.

There was no sign of life. Herault had lived above his place of work—a shop where he repaired various instruments associated with the proper working of vehicles of all kinds—cars, ships, even flipjets. The shop should have been full of machine tools, workbenches, bits and pieces of work in progress, odds and ends, and the smell of oil. It wasn't. I got in by opening the unlocked door. The place had been cleared out some time before. All that remained was the tiny office partitioned off in one corner of the shop. I switched on the light in the office and went through the drawers in the desk.

Nothing. Cleaned out to the last shred of paper. Herault was dead, all right. He'd been obliterated. Wiped off the face of the Earth.

The chair in the office was hinged so that is could be stretched into a makeshift bed. Herault had lived very closely with his work. He didn't sleep down here because he had to—his own bed was just upstairs. He used to sleep here because—occasionally—he wanted to. To be on top of the job at every moment. I'd slept here sometimes, too, but not for nearly twenty years. I extended the frame and lay down upon it.

I was too cold to be comfortable, but in time I contrived to drift off to sleep.

II

When I woke up in the morning, somebody was standing over me.

"What time is it?" I asked, trying to focus my eyes.

"Eleven o'clock," he replied, and added, "Mr. Grainger."

I sat up and looked at him hard. He was young—maybe twenty or twenty-one. He was calm and relaxed. If he'd been surprised to find me, he'd overcome his surprise by now. And he knew my name.

"People who know me," I said, "call me Grainger. Ergo, you don't know me. So how do you know who I am?"

"The last time I saw you I called you Mr. Grainger."

Seven years ago. Last time I saw Herault. There was a kid in the shop. His grandson. Parents jumped for Penaflor chasing the guy's job. Herault didn't like the guy, hadn't got on any too well with his daughter. But the kid was a different matter. Herault had taken the kid. The kid had grown up.

"Johnny," I said. "I remember you. Don't recall your father's name, though."

"Socoro," he said. "I'm Johnny Socoro." And he stuck out his hand. I shook it slowly.

"Grandfather's dead," he added.

"I know," I told him, letting my eyes move around the empty shop.

"I'd have liked to keep on running the place, but I didn't have a chance. I knew about the technical side of things, but not about the business end. And things were getting rough even before he died. No work in the port, so nothing to repair. I closed up the shop and got a job with the lines before it was too late."

"You're a spacer, then?"

"No. They don't train upship personnel here. I just look after them while they sit in the bays. I'd like to go up, but the company doesn't think much of the idea. They play pretty close to general policy. It's a dead end, but so is Earth. If you need any help in your ship I'd be grateful for anything you can offer."

"Haven't got one," I told him.

"What happened?"

"Went down in the Halcyon fringe a couple of years back. A ramrod picked me up a week or two ago. I've got nothing except a colossal debt and a few trinkets that belonged to my partner."

"You want some breakfast?"

"Sure. Shouldn't you be working, though?"

He shook his head. "Nothing down. Dead time till the *Abbenbruck* comes in from Templar tomorow."

I was surprised. Dead time in New York was new to me. That meant that the lines were using somewhere else as a center for operations. Penaflor or Valerius, I supposed. I could still remember the time when Earth was the center of the human universe, and all civilization emanated from her. And I didn't think of myself as old yet. The times, they change at a remarkable pace. New Rome had built her interstellar law, New Alexandria had cornered the market in alien knowledge, information, and data storage. It was inevitable that the spacelines would emigrate eventually to the new worlds. The hot hub stars where power was plentiful had resulted in a heavy industrial belt stretching from Penaflor to Anselm. Earth was nowhere, except where the people were. And that too had changed, in a ceaseless outward flow.

Earth just wasn't needed anymore. She had been on the decline for a hundred years. She'd nurtured the space age in her womb for over a millennium, and breast-fed the young worlds for another five centuries. But overnight, she was obsolete and dying.

Breakfast was good.

"It's all recon stuff. I'm sorry," Johnny said.

"Until last night I lived on alien salad and gruel," I replied. "It tastes great."

"I don't pull in much down at the port," he explained.

"Go to Penaflor," I said. "If Herault taught you, you'll know enough to make a mark there. For all their reputation, these heavy metal worlds aren't tough. Full of soft people living on easy money. You'll get a good ship, too, if you want to fly."

"Like I said. I don't pull in much. They won't let me work a passage, and I sure as hell can't afford a ticket."

"You could do it in short hops. Philo, Adlai, Valerius, or something like that. Get a scratch job on each world until you had the price of a jump to the next. It gets a lot easier as you go inward. The first step is the only difficult one."

"I thought of that too."

"And?"

"I'm still thinking."

"OK, Johnny," I said, feeling that I'd been bothering the kid a bit. "I'm sorry. There's no rush. Do it in your own time and your own way." Then I thought I might sound patronizing, so I shut up and concentrated on eating.

"So what are you going to do now?" he asked, as he brought the coffee.

"I don't know," I confessed. "I came out here because it was the only place I knew to come to."

"You don't know anyone else in the port?"

"If I do, they're only transients, and I wouldn't know where to find them. If I were to hang around the big bars, I'd probably recognize a few people. But they'd only be faces and names. I don't really know anybody."

"Why'd you drop ship here, instead of the inner wheel? You'd have been a hell of a lot better off. Didn't you realize what it would be like here?"

"I knew that I was going the wrong way from New Rome," I admitted. "But they offered me a lift here. And I was in the same spot you are. No cash, no prospects. Then there's Lapthorn's things. I had some vague idea about dropping them in to his old ancestral home."

"What things?"

"Just junk. But Mommy and Daddy might like to have them, now his letters don't arrive anymore. I guess they might even be harboring lingering hopes that he's still alive. I better see them."

"Do you know where they are?"

"I never met them, but he told me enough about them to make them easy to find. Two parents and one sister, still thriving last time I heard. Solidly embedded in the good old Illinois dirt. Big house and land, I believe. Last of the recon barons or something. I can get his number easily enough and tell them I have news of their long-lost-but-not-forgotten."

"You don't sound too happy about it."

"Happy? I'm delirious. What exactly am I supposed to say? Can you send me the fare to your family estate so that I can give you the full details of the *Javelin* disaster and give you a description of the rock where your son's bones lay moldering? Hell, even the cross won't be upright now I'm not there to keep standing it up."

"There's a phone downstairs," said the kid.

It was a problem that had to be faced eventually. But not now. I'd feel a real bastard asking Lapthorn senior for a touch so I could deliver his son's effects.

—You're too poor to be proud, inserted the wind.

I know it, I replied, and I must have murmured, or moved my lips, because Johnny said. "What?"

"Nothing." I said. "I talk to myself." I lapsed into silence again, thinking about the phone. Lapthorn senior, and expensive train rides.

"You mentioned a colossal debt," said Johnny. "How'd you collect that?"

"An outfit called the Caradoc Company charged me for their services in rescuing me from the rock where I went down. They took me to New Rome and got me clobbered for twenty thousand."

"Hell!" Johnny was suitably impressed. You can judge the social standing of a man even now by the sums of money he reacts to. "How did they decide on that figure?"

I shrugged. "Probably measured what they thought my gratitude ought to stretch to."

"Caradoc's the firm with the fleet in the Drift, isn't it?" said the kid. "Trying to fish for the *Lost Star*."

Inspiration descended upon me like a ton of bricks. The *Lost Star* bleep was the Lorelei of deep-space. It could be

heard all over the Halcyon Drift and quite some way outside it, but because of the warping of space inside the Drift,
its source couldn't be located. It had lured one or two good
men to an untimely death in the dark nebula. A lot of ships
whose captains had no sense and time to spare had gone in
after her. But there were no maps of the Drift, there were
dust-clouds in abundance, and the further in you went, the
more distorted was the space in which you were flying. The
core was virtually unreachable at supercee velocities. A
heavily shielded, slow-moving ship with a sound mass-
relaxation drive might reach her, if it could find her. But
nothing else stood a chance. The distortion-lesions would
tear a fast ship apart.

Ships did work in the outer Drift—but they were usually
Khorman ships. But now Caradoc had a fleet of ramrods
in there. So that was why Axel Cyran had been in such a
bad way. The Drift had worn his nerves down and the silly
fool had capped it all by homing in on *the wrong bleep*.
I could see how he might be less than happy to find that
his *Lost Star* was really a castaway pirate. Which didn't
make that twenty thousand any less of a dirty trick, though.

"They've got to be mad," I said. "They'll lose ships and
men, and even if they stood a cat in hell's chance of finding the *Lost Star*, which they don't, they'd never recover
their investment."

"Her cargo's reported to be very valuable."

"*Rumored*, not reported. Any ship that's been bleeping
for eighty years is bound to attract loose talk and romantic
notions about treasure hoards. And no cargo could be
worth the risk."

"The *Lost Star* attracted a lot of attention a year ago,
when New Alexandria offered an open contract on her
cargo. Nobody would go near her, and there was a bit of
a stir because someone tried to get the Drift declared illegal
territory to stop anyone trying. Anyhow, Caradoc is looking for privileges out in the inner wheel, and with so much
competition they have to attract attention. They're greedy,
and they reckon raising the *Lost Star* is worth a few
months of ramrod time. They've got about thirty in there,
mapping the core from all angles, and trying to narrow
down the places where the *Lost Star* might be."

"Well," I said, "I still think it's crazy. It's just a waste of resources, and I hope Caradoc regrets it. They'll pull out as soon as they start losing men. The crews will only take so much—I'm damn sure I wouldn't spend the best years of *my* life Drift-shuttling for some mindless, fat-assed company boss."

We paused in the discussion while he cleared away the breakfast remains. He looked a hell of a lot better now than he had at thirteen. He'd been a small, thin child with a sharp, not very pleasant face. He was a comfortable medium size now, with much smoother features. There were no alien shadows in his eyes. though. No remains of emotional impacts. Untouched by unhuman hand, without a doubt. I thought maybe he'd be a good engineer one day. He might be able to take Lapthorn's place if I ever did get another ship. He looked vaguely like a Lapthorn type—vulnerable to alien contact, but that might just be because he hadn't yet had the need or opportunity to throw up a shield.

"The phone," he reminded me, after a couple of minutes had passed and I'd made no move.

"Oh, yeah," I said. "The phone." I got up slowly and reluctantly.

"Mr. Grainger . . ." he said.

"Grainger," I corrected.

"Don't you have a first name?"

"No."

"Well, Grainger then . . ." He paused again.

"What d'you want?"

"When you've seen your partner's family. If you come back here, that is. I'd like to know what you intend to do. We seem to be pretty much in the same boat, and if you're going to work your way in to the hub, I'd like to come with you, if that's all right with you."

"It might be," I said. "But don't bet on it."

He thanked me kindly.

"Like I said," I emphasized, "don't bet on it. I haven't made up my mind what I'm going to do with myself yet. It might not include taking over where your last nurse left off." He looked put out, but not completely disheartened.

III

It was a woman who answered the phone—middle-aged but not letting the years get too tight a hold on her. She was alive and alert—something positive just in the manner with which she switched on the screen and looked me up and down.

"Yes?" Her voice was sharp, and sounded to me somewhat hostile—though perhaps that was my imagination.

I decided that a little cowardice in the face of the enemy might be discreet.

"I'd like to speak to Mr. William Lapthorn, if that's possible," I said.

"What about?" she asked, awkwardly.

"It's a personal matter," I said uncomfortably. I knew this beating about the bush might look bad, but I couldn't think how else to handle the old lady.

"And who are you?"

"My name's Grainger."

A deathly silence. Her face didn't change. But she knew my name. It was only my imagination again, I think, but her eyes seemed to come closer, searching me out to devour me. I brought myself under control with an abrupt effort of will, and elected to act naturally.

"It's about your son." I told her calmly. "We worked together." I hoped that the use of the last tense wouldn't send her into hysterics. But she wasn't the hysterical type.

"Tell me what you have to tell," she said.

"Is your husband there, Mrs. Lapthorn?" I persisted.

"Tell me."

"Two years ago," I said, trying not to sound too cold and mechanical, "the *Javelin* crashed in the Halcyon Drift. Your son died in the crash. I was picked up only a matter of days ago. I reached Earth yesterday. I have a few of your son's things."

The woman edged sideways on the screen. Someone else was there, easing her away so that he could get a look at me. But his own face didn't appear on my screen for a moment or two. It was obviously Lapthorn's father. The facial similarity was slight but recognizable, in the chin and mouth mostly. His eyes were completely different from his son's, though. Lapthorn's eyes had been the product of a thousand alien suns.

"Where are you?" asked William Lapthorn quietly. It struck me suddenly that he wasn't old enough to be my father. Lapthorn had come straight from the cradle to the *Fire-Eater*, but I'd worked a number of years for Herault. I'd never been quite so conscious of that age difference until now.

"I'm in New York spaceport."

"Can you get out here?"

Hesitation.

"No money?"

"No money," I agreed. It was surprisingly easy. I didn't even have to ask him.

"I'll get some to you via the nearest pickup."

"I'm in the North Area," I said.

"What's your full name?"

"Grainger. That's all there is. They have identification on file—there'll be no trouble. Tell them I dropped yesterday, then they can check with the port authority."

"Come out as fast as you can," he said. "We can't talk on the phone." The last remark, I think, was directed as much to his wife as to me.

"All right, Mr. Lapthorn," I said. "Thank you." He cut the connection midway through my thanks.

Johnny had fetched my packsack in from the office while I was phoning. He handed it to me.

"Get the money?" he asked.

"I got the money," I replied, a fraction sourly. I tapped him on the shoulder with my open palm. "Thanks for the breakfast, Johnny. I'll be back when I've seen the old man."

"You can stay as long as you like," he said.

"Sure," I said quietly.

"See you, Grainger," he called, as I went out of the door. I raised my hand in a half wave, half salute.

The pickup was just up the street and around the corner. The place was deserted. Even though it was late morning, I felt uncomfortably alone in a city which had once been all activity. Maybe, I thought, the whole North Area stays in bed when Johnny's line doesn't have a ship down.

At the pickup I dialed through to the Illinois cybernet and announced my identity. The New York net checked and confirmed my identity, and the two decided after a momentary conference that I really was entitled to be collecting money on the Lapthorn account. A credit card, punched and banded, oozed out of a slot and flopped down onto the counter. I inspected it, but couldn't make head nor tail of the code. That sort of thing tends to change very quickly.

I tapped out a query on the keyboard, asking how much the card was carrying. The printout said six hundred. That was high, unless the unitary cost index had been untied from pay levels in the state. I asked, and it hadn't. Two and two still made four, and six hundred was enough to take me a lot further than Illinois. I could flipjet to Chicago and ride a train to Lapthorn's for a tenth of it.

I suppose it seemed logical to the elder Lapthorn that he should be free with his petty cash, but his excessive charity left me unmoved. What's he trying to buy? I wondered.

—He can't buy you for a lousy six hundred, said the wind, with something that sounded remarkably like a sneer. You're worth twenty thousand.

And two hundred a month to the insurance company to make sure I don't get off too lightly, I supplied. I wonder what sort of a policy they got. No one would insure me to go deep-spacing on the rim. But that's irrelevant. Six hundred is a lot of loose change.

—The guy knows you're down and out. He knows you were his son's soulmate. He thinks you've made a pilgrimage to Earth just to deliver the news and the mortal remains. So should he leave you without the price of a meal? He's trying to help you.

Thanks, I said. You're a great comfort to a spaceman in distress.

—Any time, the wind assured me.

I reflected that the wind was getting to sound like me. He was digging in deeper all the time. I wondered about the day when I became more him than me, but he didn't comment on the matter, leaving it to my imagination.

From the pickup to the inland jet field was only a matter of a couple of miles, but I called a taxi. I figured that if I owed William Lapthorn anything for his generous handout, it was all due speed in getting to him.

On the flipjet, I began to wonder about the people I was going to see. What sort of parents could blend halves of themselves into a Lapthorn? He was an odd combination of vulnerability and indestructibility. What sort of home could have generated his phenomenal appetite for strangeness and unhumanity?

I hadn't seen enough of Lapthorn's parents to make any sensible judgment. The mother austere, the father efficient —superficial estimates only. Perhaps, I thought, they had been too efficient and therefore distant—starved the atmosphere of uncertainty and anticipation. I visualized the young Lapthorn living an automated existence, anchored in an endless static present, with no perspective in either memory or forethought. Had a debt built up that he had needed to discharge? Maybe so—but if that had been the whole truth, the star-worlds would have burned him up within weeks. What made Lapthorn last so long? He was twenty—Johnny Socoro's age—when the *Fire-Eater* first touched down on alien dirt. He was thirty-five when the *Javelin* went down. Fifteen years is a lot of time to be constantly inhaling alien air and alien thought. I was a good deal older and made of hard stone, but it was a wonder that I survived. How much more of a wonder that Lapthorn was still unhurt, unconquered, and undiminished.

Could the same be said of his parents? Unhurt, unconquered, undiminished? Were they just the same now as the day he left for deep-space? Seventeen years might not even have touched them in a stable, mechanical environment. For all the character they'd add to themselves in seventeen blind years, they might have waved good-bye the day before yesterday.

All this wasn't wholly romance. It had always seemed to me that this was the way the rich chose to live—in time-less isolation, protected from all harm by the mechanization of their homes and their lives. They atrophied, mentally and socially, because their brains were no longer used.

—You're afraid of these people.

I'm not afraid. They can't hurt me. But I don't like them. I can't.

—You haven't even seen them.

It doesn't matter precisely who or what they are. I don't like them. I don't like what I am to them, or what they are to me. We're related, through Lapthorn, and that's a farce. Because the Lapthorn I know and the Lapthorn they know are two completely different people. Because Lapthorn and I are two completely different people. We don't fit—none of us. Not even if the connecting piece was still here and alive could I like Lapthorn's parents or they like me. It's futile.

—You aren't exactly a *capable* entity, are you, Grain-ger? Blocked by confusion and lack of understanding at every mental step. Can't you even perform a simple task like returning your partner's junk to its rightful resting place? Is this your own personal failing or is it a character-istic of your race?

All right, I conceded, there are fields in which I'm not very capable. So what? I imagine that my peculiar incapac-ities are mine and mine only, but I can't speak for the human race. Their capabilities or lack of them are their own affair.

—Why don't you use a first name, Grainger?

Because I haven't got one.

—I know you don't know of one. I know your unknown mother and father didn't leave you one as a parting gift. But that's not the only way to come by names, is it? Why not give *yourself* a name? Do yourself a favor.

I don't need another name.

—You don't want another name. It would demean you to use one. It might seem as though you had an identity, as though you were a member of the human race, as though you really existed instead of being a legend of the rim stars.

So suddenly you're an expert on human psychology.

—I'm an expert on *you*. Grainger, and I'm learning more all the time. I'm right inside you. I'm with you every decision you take. I'm riding your every thought, and feeling everything you feel. This isn't the most comfortable of minds to live in, my friend. I would appreciate it greatly if you could get it sorted out a little. Come to terms with yourself and the universe.

If I'd known you wanted to reform me, I replied, I'd never have let you in. You're stuck with me, and if you don't like it, then it's too bad. I don't give a damn whether or not my mind is your idea of the Garden of Eden. If you don't like riding my thoughts, get off.

—I'm with you till you die. You know that.

Well, you're with the me you know and apparently don't think much of. You can't change me. You can live in my mind, but you can't alter it. So forget it. I don't need your help to run my affairs. You're welcome to stay, just so long as you keep quiet.

—I'm not sure that I can comply with that, mine host. I think you occasionally need reminding when you act the fool. And I think you might need my help one day.

I'll do without, thanks.

—We'll see.

Do I consult you as if you were an oracle, or do we take a democratic vote? I remarked.

He observed the sarcasm, and shut up.

There was a slightly foul taste in my mouth, caused by too much thinking. Silent conversation with the wind was engrossing. I roused myself to take note of my surroundings and came back to the land of the not-yet-dead.

IV

The Lapthorn estate was just beyond Aurora. The train stopped at a tiny town that looked just as deserted as the spaceport. All of Earth seemed to have gone to sleep.

There was a car waiting at the station, with a small sandy-haired guy driving. He didn't introduce himself, but I assumed he must be the hired hand, and that the Lapthorns were all at home, anxiously preparing for the arrival of the next best thing to the prodigal son. The car was a nice, newly sprayed skyrider that was perfectly smooth on her cushion. A lot of these fancy floating jobs are no real improvement on groundhogs as far as jumping and jerking are concerned. But some poor engineer had put his heart into making this one behave as the advertising material said it would. That sort of thing had been Herault's claim to a meaningful existence.

The house was big, and the grounds suitably impressive. The grandeur of empty land should be losing its status and becoming a fraction ridiculous now the starward flow had reduced the population by seventy or eighty percent, but a bit of empty Earth was still worth noticing. The grass would be Andean, of course, and the trees from Australia or Alaska. Ninety-nine percent of the northeastern states had been under concrete at one time with nothing living free except flies, rats, and humans, plus other minor vermin. All this was reclaimed, like the food which had made the Lapthorn family its fortune in the first place.

The interior décor was fabulous, and the polite atmosphere you could feel between your fingers. It was ten minutes before anyone said anything to me which wasn't a socially respectable synthetic. Even then we took time getting down to the real heart of the matter.

There were four of us seated in a circle. I'd been offered food and drink and—for the sake of convenience—met the offers with a blanket refusal. I'd been welcomed and thanked about three times. So now we reached the guts of the story. Lapthorn junior was dead and I wasn't. How, why, and what the hell else was there?

Mrs. Lapthorn sat on my left, leaning forward like a predatory bird waiting to snatch up the words as they fell. William Lapthorn sat opposite, looking majestically relaxed. The Lapthorn lips were held in a straight line—not taut or limp, just restrained from evidencing any reaction. Eve Lapthorn—the sister—sat to my right, waiting without having yet decided what she was going to do or say. I had the odd sensation that she was the only living thing in the room.

I told them about my first meeting with Michael Lapthorn—it was a continual effort to refer to him by his first name. I'd rarely called him by any name at all—you don't have to when you work that closely together—but I'd always thought of him by his surname. Herault, of course, had first brought us together. I had some money, he had some money. Separately, we amounted to nothing. Together, we added up to a cheap spaceship, which was what we both wanted. We hadn't bothered about such things as compatibility—in such a manner are marriages of convenience made.

I told them briefly of our years in space. I made nothing whatsoever of the gulf which existed between Lapthorn's nature and mine, nor that between Lapthorn's needs and ambitions and mine. They'd have formed their own ideas about that from his letters, and the only thing I knew about those was that there were a lot of them. I didn't want to shatter any illusions, whatever they might be.

I told them how the *Javelin* had run into trouble because of dust carrying either distorted space or radiation out from the Drift, while we were en route for Hallsthammer from Adadict, and been drawn back into the Drift with the cloud. I didn't tell them that the idiot who'd plotted a course which shaved the Drift so fine was me, trying to economize on fuel. Nor did I point out that if it hadn't been for Lapthorn we wouldn't have *been* short of fuel, nor even in the Drift region. I gave them the pure facts, and let them assign their own blame.

I told them how the controls had seized once we were into the Drift, and how I'd been unable to slow her down until the distortion had ripped our shield away and bled our power so that we didn't have a hope of getting out again. I described our one last drop—how I'd searched for a star and headed into the system with all the optimism I could muster, and how I'd contrived to put her down on a world which just *might* sustain life. I couldn't convey to them just how lucky I had been, because they were concentrating their attention on how unlucky Lapthorn had been. Somehow, he'd kept the piledriver alive despite the drain. I had impulse barely sufficient to get the *Javelin* down. But not in one piece. We had nowhere near the blast required to balance her and set her down feather-light. We went in hard and low. I tried to straighten her out, but it was no good. One end or the other was bound to take the impact and break. It was the back end. Michael Lapthorn died.

Amen.

Silence from the audience. No comment until they'd mulled it over. Mother didn't trust me and didn't like me. It was my fault, by her standards, I'd been entrusted with the life of her son, and I'd been careless enough to break her toy. Too bad. Father, on the other hand, accepted the inevitability of events. At all costs show no hostility to poor Grainger, because it wouldn't be sporting. No blame to be laid at all. Keep that mouth straight. Eve was just a little lost. Perhaps having trouble remembering dear Michael. She was very young when he left home. A little guilty, maybe, because she couldn't remember him. She thought all this ought to mean more to her, but it didn't quite fit in.

All this I knew before anyone opened his mouth.

"You're not at all as I expected you to be," said the old man, eventually. OK, I thought, avoid the subject altogether. Talk about me instead, if you'd rather.

"I'm sorry," I said.

"In Michael's letters you seem to be quite a different man."

"I've spent the last two years alone on a dead rock," I reminded him.

"It goes deeper than that," he said. "You don't seem to be the kind of man my son would idolize."

Idolize? I wondered what on Earth Lapthorn had written about me.

"You were a kind of hero, as far as my son was concerned," he clarified. It was news to me.

"You mean his early letters," I said dubiously. "He was young then. . . ."

"Oh, no," the elder Lapthorn interrupted me. "*All* his letters. In fifteen years, his opinion didn't change. He always thought the same about you, wrote about you in the same way. His letters didn't change."

His letters didn't change. Fifteen years of deep-space—of filling up with new knowledge, new experience, new feeling, and his letters home didn't change. I swear that the Lapthorn who died on that rock wasn't the Lapthorn that left home. By no means. And now his father sits in his unchanging armchair in his unchanging drawing room and tells me that he couldn't tell the difference.

"I don't understand," I said pointlessly.

"It must have been rough," said Eve Lapthorn. "After the ship went down."

"The wind kept me company," I said—softly, whimsically.

"You seem to be all right now, though," the older woman supplied.

"I'm fine," I said. "It wasn't too bad—I was a bit hungry, but I'm over that now." Sheer courage and nobility shone out of me. Oh, it was nothing, really. You can say that, once it's a couple of weeks behind you and you're sitting in someone's drawing room.

"The things you brought back," said the old woman. "Where are they?"

"In my packsack," I said. "I left it in the hall." I got up, but they made me sit down again, and Eve brought it in, opening it as she crossed the room. All she found on top was my dirty shirt. I stood up and took it from her.

I took out Lapthorn's personal possessions from the bottom of the bag.

There was his wristwatch, his identity papers, and his

sunglasses. That ended the utility section. There were four bits of rock—each uniquely patterned but quite worthless; a pair of wings from a big arthropoid; and some small items of alien jewelry—presents from various people.

"Is this all?" said his father.

What did you expect, I almost said, holiday snapshots? Lapthorn didn't need crude images—his memories were *alive*. This was just junk.

"We don't carry much aboard ship," I tried to explain. "It's not like a liner where they have space to spare and fuel to waste. These were just personal items—just for the sake of *having* a few personal possessions. I'm sorry there's nothing here of even sentimental value, but your son just didn't have anything *concrete* that he valued that much."

"What do you mean by nothing concrete?" asked Eve.

"I mean he carried things in his mind," I said. Inadequately. How could I explain?

"We have his letters," said his mother. Implying: we could have done without *you*. You needn't have bothered.

"That's right," said the old man. "The letters contain much more meaning than we could hope to find in the contents of his pockets. Would you like to see them?"

Who are you trying to kid? I thought. You wouldn't understand a meaning if it were six feet tall. But his offer surprised me. Admitted to the inner sanctum of Lapthorn family feeling as regards the late lamented.

"No thank you," I said. Mother hadn't liked the idea either. She looked pleased when I refused.

The family affair was winding down. I could feel it. We had all done our duty by the dead man. What should be said to assuage social responsibility had been said, and there was nothing left. My presence would soon become a burden, but they wouldn't think of letting me leave yet. After all (they said) they wanted a chance to get to know me. We had so much to talk about. Like hell. But they didn't even see that it was nonsense.

Feeling trapped, I stayed for dinner. It was, at least, another meal which wouldn't put a strain on my pocket

V

I intended to leave as soon as possible the next day. I took a shower before breakfast. My clothes had been cleaned while I slept. I grabbed the packsack as soon as we'd eaten, bid a hurried farewell, and bolted for the gate. The steamroller tactics shook the elder Lapthorns but Eve was quick to volunteer to drive me to the station. I could hardly refuse.

"What's all the hurry?" she wanted to know. "I thought you'd be glad to rest up for a few days."

"I might be," I told her. "But not here. Uncomfortable. Got to get a job, anyhow."

"That won't be easy."

"It's necessary," I said flatly. She gave me a questioning look. I told her about the Caradoc Company's little joke.

"You didn't say anything about that last night."

"Why should I? It's nothing to do with your brother. Hey, you drive like a spacepilot." One hand on the wheel, the other on the gear lever. Most drivers use two hands to the wheel most of the time, but a pilot's used to operating two sets of controls—one with each hand. She ignored the comment about her driving, and said: "We might have been able to help."

"I suppose Daddy would have handed over twenty thousand without a qualm," I said sarcastically. "Just for his son's old times' sake."

"We have some contacts in the starship line," she said.

"They wouldn't take me on as a liner jockey," I said. "I'm a free trader. But thanks anyway. How does the old

44

man happen to have contacts in that direction? Play golf with the liner men?" The comments annoyed her, and she didn't attempt to explain. She just said: "They're not his contacts, they're mine." She went no further, and I assumed she had a spacer boyfriend. If I'd restrained my wit at this point and let her talk, I could have saved a great deal of misunderstanding later. But I didn't.

I said: "Look. You don't have to worry about me. I'm no different from three or four hundred other drifters hanging around the port looking to pick up a ship. I'm nothing to you except that I happened to be on the spot when your brother died. That doesn't make me the hero he thought I was. It doesn't make me a sort of poor cousin to his family. You don't owe me anything for his watch and his eyeshades. Not anymore, anyhow—Daddy made sure I got my blood money. Enough for a passage to Seymour. I could work my way back into a paying job inside a year."

"But it wouldn't be paying you," she pointed out. "It would only be paying Caradoc."

And that, of course, was the big crunch.

"OK," I said. "So Caradoc owns my soul. Tough. Better than rotting out my days on that black mountain."

"Are you really the best pilot in the galaxy, Mr. Grainger?" she asked. I couldn't tell whether or not she was trying to be funny.

"No, I'm not," I said. "There are a thousand as good or better. I just happen to be one of the ones they talk about. It wasn't my flying that got us a reputation, it was the crazy places your brother conned me into flying to."

"Could a better pilot have avoided that crash?"

Dangerous ground. Take great care. "Nobody could," I said. "She was just snatched out of my hands at twenty-five thou. The dust would have run off the shield—it was only light. But the lesion, or whatever it was, never gave me a chance."

"You've dealt with dust and distortion before, I suppose," she said, ruminatively.

"Of course I have. Look, I didn't kill your brother. I *couldn't* have saved him. Nobody could. OK, so I'm not the best pilot there is. But I'm one hell of a lot better than what the schools turn out to nurse the liners. I didn't spend my time learning what to do if the chain in the captain's lavatory breaks. I spent my formative years learning about engines, and learning how to *feel* a ship. When the *Javelin's* controls seized, I damn near had a heart attack in sympathy. Now, do you believe me?"

"I believe you," she said levelly. "Where can I find you if I can put a job your way?"

"Forget it," I said.

"You don't want any help, do you?"

"No."

"It's not that you're too proud, either. You just don't want anything to do with *us*. You want to forget us—wipe us out of your memory."

"I've done what I came to do. I don't want to be your brother's hero or your brother's ghost. I gave you back his stuff. He's dead—I have to carry on. Lapthorn's *dead*. He doesn't figure anymore."

"Did you *like* my brother?"

There was a pause, during which she settled the skyrider beside the monorail platform. I climbed out, and she got out too, following me. The train wasn't due for ten minutes. She wasn't letting go.

"We were very different," I said.

"Did you like him?" she persisted.

"Of course I liked him. We crammed ourselves into the same little hull for fifteen years, didn't we? D'you think we could have stood that if we couldn't stand the sight of each other?"

Maybe not. Fifteen years is a long time. But the first part was a lie. No, I didn't like Lapthorn. Never did. Never could. But I wasn't going to tell her that.

She walked a few yards up the platform, then turned to face me. It's odd how you can half ignore someone at a distance of two feet—contrive always to look past them or around them. But at five or six yards they're in your sights. You can't look past them. You have to recognize them. I had to look at Eve Lapthorn now—maybe for the first time.

She wasn't pretty by home planet standards, though she'd have looked good out on the rim. She looked a lot like her father, but not too much like her brother. She had her father's cool efficiency of manner, his firm expression, his matter-of-fact stance. There was some of Michael Lapthorn in her, maybe, but she didn't *move* like Lapthorn. She didn't have his orientation to the world around her. She had direction and momentum, but all one way. No sideways glances, no curiosity. A set mind.

"Where can I get in touch with you?" she asked again.

I gave her Herault's address.

"I'll be there for a while," I said. "I'm staying with a downship maintenance man named Johnny Socoro. But if I get a job I'll be leaving Earth without saying any good-byes."

"I'll be in touch," she said, and she meant it. Then she turned her back and walked away. The skyrider lifted gracefully and casually slid back onto the empty road. She didn't wave good-bye.

I caught a connecting train at Chicago. Six hours as opposed to half an hour by flight, but I wasn't in a hurry anymore, and I could afford to eke out the Lapthorn donation in a sensible fashion now it was all mine and free of any obligation.

When I got back to Herault's place I rang the doorbell but got no answer. Johnny, I remembered, would be working on the *Abbenbruck*. I had no idea what time he'd be home. I dumped the packsack in the shop and wandered off to find something to eat.

Recon food still tasted pretty good. Earthers who can't afford real food more than once a month claim they can taste the algae and the respun protein no matter what they do to it, but Earthers always complain about their mistreated bellies. I spent too much of my life on gruel to complain about anything with taste.

While I was eating, a spacer who'd been drinking in the bar came over to my table and sat down. I peered at him for a moment or two, and then recognized him as a crewman from the p-shifter which had escorted me under arrest from Hallsthammer to New Rome, and then given me a lift to Earth. He hadn't spoken to me on board the ship, but I'd seen him a couple of times in the corridors and at feeding time.

"Caradoc played pretty dirty with you, didn't they?" he said. This masterpiece of understatement didn't seem to me to be a diplomatic way to open a sociable chat, but I grunted agreement.

"It was Cyran," he said. "He pushed it on our skipper.
HQ backed him, but if you ask me there was more to it
than that. Max—our skipper—might square you with HQ
and talk them into giving you a job where you can work
out that twenty thousand. It'd be cheaper than working it
off out of another company's wage packet. And Cyran
can't kick up any more dirt—he's still pussyfooting around
in the Drift looking for the mermaids."

"Don't you think the joke's gone stale by now?" I said.
"I wouldn't work for Caradoc after this."

He shrugged his shoulder apologetically. "Yeah, I realize it's a hell of a thing to suggest—go work for the guy
who just stabbed you in the back. But it's the only way
you'll survive that debt. I'm only trying to help."

"Everybody is trying to help me," I said. "And thank
you all. But I'd need my head examined if I let Caradoc
pull a trick like this. Slave labor isn't nice. My vocation in
life is *not* to push ramrods through the filth that accumu-
lates in the Halcyon Drift. Or are you intending to use me
in the next publicity stunt? Like the circumnavigation of
the universe, or a brief trip on mega-p six? Or maybe the
conquest of Earth?"

He got the hint, drained his drink, and got up to leave.

"If you change your mind," he said, "the *Tahini* will be
back on Earth in a week's time, on the standard shuttle
run."

There was no animosity in his voice—no injured pride.
He really had thought I'd been badly done to. And he
really had thought that the only way out was to feed the
hand that bit me.

"Thanks," I said to him as he left. Despite all the thanks
I was handing out lately, I seemed to be letting go of very
little real gratitude.

VI

Three days later, delArco turned up on Johnny's door-step. He was a big man—not far off six feet, I judged, with a strongly built frame. He moved smoothly, too, and not slowly. I couldn't imagine anyone picking a fight with him. His hair was showing streaks of gray, but he was younger than I was. Living on Earth had aged him faster.

"Johnny's not here," I told him. "There's a ship down."

"I'm Nick delArco, Grainger, I came to see you."

"I've never heard of you," I said.

"That's right," he agreed.

"Did Eve Lapthorn send you?"

"She told me where to find you. She works for me. But she didn't send me. My backers asked me to locate you."

We were still standing in the doorway. With a slight movement of his body he indicated that he wanted to come in, and I moved aside. We went upstairs to the rooms above the shop. He made himself comfortable in the chair I'd been using to watch the HV set. It was still on, but he ignored it. I didn't bother to switch it off, just seated myself in another chair and waited for him to move around to face me.

"You seem hostile, Grainger," he remarked. "What have I done?"

"Nothing."

"Are you at all interested in what I have to say?"

"Don't know until I hear it. I could be."

His eyes fixed on mine and held them. "You don't have to be grateful," he said. "I'm not trying to help you out.

49

I'm just trying to hire a pilot. You're available and you have a big reputation."

"That's rim talk," I said. "They don't reckon me around these parts."

"You worked for New Alexandria once. They think highly of you."

Which was nice of them, I suppose.

"I'm listening," I said.

"I've built a ship and I've been commissioned to take her on her maiden voyage. I'd like you to be the pilot. It's a rather special ship. She's flown in atmosphere but that's nothing. She'll need a lot of handling to fly where she's intended to. We need a better pilot than we can find in the inner wheel."

"What's so special about the ship?" I asked.

"It's a composite. New Alexandria has been working for several years on a synthesis of human and Khormon technology and theory. They've had a number of contractors working on the various technological possibilities thrown out by the fusion. This ship is one. The New Alexandrians are hoping they can start a new scientific revolution—get things moving again. Because of the flow of people through the star-worlds, things have been stagnant for a long while. Even before the migration, real scientific advance was at a standstill. New shapes and new sizes, but no new principles. We thought we had them all. But the Khormon synthesis has added one or two new angles.

"We've built a ship which can really fly, Grainger. Not like a bullet, but like a bird. She's jointed and musculated. She has the most complete and most sensitive nerve-net any mechanical device has ever had. She can react fast and she can absorb the energy of her own reaction. This bird can maneuver at speeds in excess of twenty thou."

"That's not possible," I said. Nothing ought to be able to turn even the merest fraction with anything like that momentum behind it. Any ship would break in two under the strain, joints or no joints. Whichever of the various gimmicks you employ to beat the Einstein barrier—tachyonic transfer, probability shift, dimensional hopping—it all amounts to the same thing—if anything gets in your way you have to go through it. *You can't turn.* Not at twenty thousand cee.

"It is now," said delArco calmly.

"You've not actually tried it?"

"She maneuvers well in atmosphere."

"So do dragonflies. You want me to fly her the first time you try her in deep-space."

"That's right."

"I can see why you need me. No liner jockey would touch it with a barge pole. I'm not sure that I will. Nor anyone else with any sense. It sounds like one hell of a risk to me."

"I'm going up with her. I built her."

"So you take a pride in your work," I said. "Very commendable. Give the shipbuilder a gold star. But you didn't design her, did you?"

"I didn't have to. The best brains on New Alexandria put the blueprints together. Big money from New Alexandria financed the ship. They know she'll fly and so do I."

"What's the drive?"

"Mass-relaxation."

"And you have the fineness of control to hit twenty thou? That's a remarkable achievement, if it's true."

"I said she'd turn at twenty thou. She'll fly straight at fifty. This is a *real* ship, Grainger, not a clockwork tin can. She's only plated with metal—a kind of exoskeleton. She's not solid. The rest of her is organic chain molecules —plastics of all types. The plastic and the metal are knitted by organo-metallic synapses, which are damn near perfect. Piloting this ship will be like nothing you've ever done before. The neuronic linkup is so good your body will become part of the body of the ship. Your mind will be the mind of the ship. You fly by feel, don't you? Well, you've never really felt a ship. You can feel the ship's skin, but it isn't *your* skin. You can feel the power in the drive, but it's outside you—down in the belly. In my ship the hull will be your skin, the drive will be *inside* you. The sensory hookup is that good. And in consequence her reactivity is way in advance of anything there's ever been before. She can turn, she can move in flight. She can cope with dust, with distortion. The only thing which will bother her is wide-beam radiation. Tight-beam she can dodge. Grainger, this ship can run an obstacle course at five hundred cee. She can go through mazes at a thousand."

"If pigs had wings they could maybe do the same."

"Is that all you have to say?"

"No. What makes you think I could learn to fly a ship like that? It's like nothing I've ever encountered before. Why am I any more use to you than the next man?"

"Because you fly *naturally*. You fly with the ship. You don't leave the dirty work to machines. You *are* a pilot, and the Penaflor men *aren't*. They're carriage-pushers."

"Well," I said, "we agree on that if on nothing else."

"And you've seen more dirty space than anyone else we can reach. You know what we have to face if this ship is going to live up to its purpose and go where no other ship can."

That, I suppose, was true. There's a distortion and dirt in plenty out on the rim. It isn't all collected in the cesspits like the Halcyon Drift. I'd seen far more than my share. Blame Lapthorn and his trailblazing for that.

"What's your offer?" I asked delArco.

"New Alexandria will pay off your twenty thousand tomorrow, if you sign a two-year contract to pilot this ship, under my captaincy."

I got instantly suspicious. "And if I resign, the twenty thousand gets slapped right back on, in its entirely and with all strings attached?"

"Yes."

"Come off it," I said. "That's not hiring me. That's buying me lock, stock, and barrel. How can I work with that hanging over me like the sword of bloody Damocles. That's slave labor, without even a chance to run away. You know I can't touch a deal like that."

"I know you can't afford not to. Any other way it'll take the rest of your life to pay off that ticket. It's not all that bad—your rights as contracted labor are protected by the Law of New Rome. You're not a slave, except to that twenty thousand, if you don't try to get rid of it."

"I have the distinct feeling that the Law of New Rome has gone bad while I've been away," I said. "Every time I hear it quoted these days it sounds bent. Your offer stinks. I wouldn't touch it if I couldn't get another job as long as I live."

"I'm sorry, Grainger," he said, "but this comes from over my head. The New Alexandrians were very particular about who they wanted to pilot their ship and under what conditions. This is the offer, and in monetary terms it's very generous. And it isn't as if you were being sent into a uranium mine. Other people will ride this ship with you. Me for one, and at least two more. We're going to be exposed to exactly the same risks as you are—and you'll be the one the rest of us are depending on. I think it's a good offer."

"Well, I think you're a fool, if you really mean that. When I want to give somebody a two-year lease on my soul, I'll contact the devil direct. He gives plenty much the same deal, and he thought of it first."

After the big man had gone—departed in something of a bad mood—I transferred myself to the seat he'd vacated and resumed staring mindlessly at the HV. I didn't want to think too hard about the offer, in case I conned myself into taking it.

for ... . There's don't-care. But it has to be used
with ... loan ...
... with ... drew ... in its more emphatic ... the
... and the world, ... in its assault significance ... all
... the ... of ...

VII

—Well, Golden Boy, said the whisper, this is your big chance.

It could well be a big bust. Suicide.

—New Alexandria doesn't make mistakes. This isn't the Caradoc Company.

You don't know a damn thing about New Alexandria. You can't possibly judge.

—I know what you know. And my judgments based on what you know are no less valid than yours. In fact, I'd back mine against yours any time.

And you think that I ought to take this crazy job.

—I judge that you have no reasonable choice. It's a risk, but so is everything else.

Even assuming that the ship can fly, which seems to me to be unlikely, there's still the matter of my being *able* to fly it. I've never flown a mass-relaxation ship before. Contrary to what appears to be public belief, I didn't fly the *Fire-Eater* and the *Javelin* solely on intuition. I used all the mechanical aids at my disposal. And I had to be taught—well and carefully taught—by someone who knew all about spaceships. Who can teach me about this one?

—You're a big boy now. You can look after yourself. If you need any help, I'll be around.

So now you're the galaxy's number one spacepilot as well?

—No. I only live here.

That's extremely amusing. Incredibly funny. You have obviously reached my sense of humor during your internal

54

perambulations. Please don't overuse it—it has to be kept well under control.

—There may be only one body at the controls of the ship, said the wind, ignoring my sarcasm completely, but there'll be two minds. Two minds are better than one.

Like hell. How do you expect me to fly the ship if you keep interrupting me?

—I won't interrupt you, he explained patiently. I'll simply learn while you learn. I have a different point of view. Between us, we'll learn how to fly the ship faster than you could if you were alone. And you still can't afford to pass up this job.

Even at the terms I've been offered?

—The terms enable you to achieve your desired object —get rid of the debt to Caradoc. They aren't easy terms, but twenty thousand is never easy.

I get you, I thought dolefully. It might pay normally not to bet when you can't afford to lose, but when the occasion comes when you can't afford not to win, it's time to think again.

I was being slowly convinced when Johnny interrupted me, and allowed me to forget the argument for the time being.

"You know that guy delArco you saw yesterday?" he said.

"Yeah."

"He's outside, in a car. I've been talking to him. He's waiting for us."

"For *us?*"

"That's right." The kid looked at me in the face, almost defiantly. "He thinks there might be a job for me on his ship."

"As what?" I asked him. "Cook?"

"Crewman."

"Marvelous," I remarked, with even the sarcasm turning lukewarm through lack of enthusiasm. The possibility occurred to me that delArco had offered the kid a job as an added inducement to me, although I couldn't see any reason for him to assume that I cared particularly about Johnny Socoro. Maybe he just happened to want a spare crewman. Maybe Johnny was good at his job. Maybe

Johnny was the only shipworker in port crazy enough to risk taking the berth.

We went down to the car. Waiting in the front passenger seat was Nick delArco. The car was the Lapthorn skyrider, and its driver was Eve Lapthorn.

She smiled at me; delArco looked less than delighted by the sour expression on my face. It obviously hadn't been his idea to bring her along.

"Get in, Mr. Grainger," she said, "and we'll take you to see your bird."

"You can call me Grainger," I offered, with all due magnanimity. "I presume you've already met Johnny."

She flashed Johnny a nice smile, and nodded agreement. Johnny looked at me, and I propelled him gently into the back seat of the car, then followed him.

"Mr. delArco told me you work for him," I said to Eve. "I didn't realize you were his chauffeur."

"I have a small interest in the ship," she replied, but didn't say what it was.

"Am I going to have Lapthorns on my back till the day I die?" I asked harshly, letting some of my temper slip. I glanced sideways at Johnny, who'd jumped slightly at the venom in the remark.

Eve blushed, and rammed the car into a sort of kangaroo leap which lifted us from the ground and threw us into a jerky flight. The engine groaned, and she settled us into horizontal by brute force, with a reasonable helping of willful ignorance. The ride was rough for a couple more minutes while she piled on the power going around bends, but she calmed down before anyone's hair had a chance to turn white.

"Have you considered my offer?" asked delArco, turning around to face us, Johnny opened his mouth to reply, but I interrupted him.

"We're both considering your propositions," I said. "Neither of us knows enough yet to be sure. After we've seen the ship we'll be in a better position to decide."

He seemed perfectly satisfied by that, and Johnny was content to let me do the talking for both of us.

"What's the name of the ship, Mr. delArco?" asked Johnny.

"The *Hooded Swan*," Eve answered for him. "It was my idea."

"That's a strange name," he said, hesitating slightly over the word "strange."

"It was another name for the bird called a dodo," she explained.

"You have an odd sense of humor," I remarked. "A lot of people would think that's a bad name for a ship."

"But you don't believe in bad luck," she said.

"No."

"Then it's all right. In any case, it will be conventional ships which eventually wind up as dead as the dodo. Not this ship."

"Don't count your dodos before they're hatched," I said dryly. She went red again.

Eve took the car into the old yards. There were newer, better yards on the south side that still saw a certain amount of work, but these were deserted. There hadn't been a liner built here in twenty years, and even the private concerns didn't bother with them now. There was better accommodation available for anyone who thought that he simply had to build on Earth. There was the sound of hammering and tinkering emanating from one tower, but it sounded lonely and distant. It was probably somebody messing about with his car. In the bays over the far side of the yards I could see three yachts and a couple of obsolete cargo ships. The yachts were probably strictly for joyriding, and the cargo ships either antiques or scrap. There were a couple of people wandering around, but they were too aimless to be workers. Sightseers, perhaps, or scavengers. They seemed to me like vermin crawling in the corpse of the yards. It had never been more evident that Earth was *dead*.

We were nearly two miles out in the complex before we came to our destination. The yard delArco was using was about the most isolated he could find. It was dead quiet. The yard had a high wall, with no overt signs of occupancy, but I could see that the tower within held something more than dust. In addition, there were men on top of the tower—not obvious to the casual glance, but visible if you looked hard enough.

The gateway was guarded too. We were admitted

through a small hatch in the door, but only after delArco
had been scrutinized and identified. I wondered whether
all this was a product of delArco's hitherto unsuspected
flair for the melodramatic, or whether the New Alexandrians really thought their project warranted this kind of
cloak-and-dagger treatment.

"Are there bobby traps as well?" I asked.

DelArco nodded absently, while he searched for the right
key to open the outer door of the tower. He had to find
two more for the inner doors, but we finally made it into
the inner sanctum, where we were greeted with false
warmness by some guy who'd been waiting for us for
some time. I shook his hand without looking at him or
hearing his name. My eyes were on the ship.

It's one thing to sit on a chair in front of an HV screen,
with the remains of lunch still on the table and cigarette
ash on the carpet, and talk about a ship. It's quite a different matter to stand underneath her belly and look up
at her.

In Johnny Socoro's house, the *Hooded Swan* had been
an abstraction—a ship that couldn't fly, an extravagant
dream. Here, in the dimness of her construction tower,
she was a living thing. A reality, full of substance and
beauty.

I'm not a Lapthorn, to fall in love with a ship. But I'm
a spaceman. Ships are my life, my outer skin, my power
and my glory.

When I see a ship, I don't lose my mind in an orgiastic
swell of emotion, like six out of seven bad spacers. I'm
not overwhelmed by the loveliness and sheer majesty of
a ship. But I know these things for what they are. I can
see them. And the *Hooded Swan* was lovely. Make no
mistake about that.

A ship's performance in deep-space isn't necessarily connected to her *presence* on the ground, or lack of it, but a
spacer's confidence. DelArco was right. This ship wasn't
a bullet—not a steel worm or a giant metal egg on stilts.
This ship was a bird. It was built to move. I hadn't fully
appreciated before what delArco had implied when he
said the ship was jointed. This ship was like a living being
—a bird with feathers of shiny metal. A deep-space alba-
tross. Liners are built to look graceful, to look proud, to

look powerful. But the real paucity of their ambition couldn't be appreciated until you compared them to the *Hooded Swan*. Eve Lapthorn was right, too. This ship *might* make rigid ships obsolete. If she flew as well as she looked. If she flew at all.

"She looks good," I said calmly.

They smiled, because they knew I was understating deliberately. They'd watched me looking at her.

"Shut your mouth, Johnny," I said, to break the silence. The kid was far too obviously impressed. He'd spent all his working life getting to know the inside and outside of liners far too well. He'd only just realized what a starship was.

"Well?" said delArco.

"I'd like a look at the controls," I said. "I think we're all agreed that it's very pretty."

"It's wonderful," said Johnny.

"Maybe so," I said. "But being the fairest of them all won't help her fly in deep-space."

The initial impact of seeing her was wearing off, and I was slowly beginning to suspect that it was all too good to be true. She looked just *too* beautiful to take on the rigors of deep-space. Deep-space is empty and desolate and—above all—lifeless. The *Hooded Swan* suggested *life* in her every line, but not toughness, not sheer brute strength. Could she really cope?

The first sight of the controls startled me. The old *Javelin* hadn't been to difficult to feel, because in terms of control there weren't too many fancy gadgets. Just a pair of manipulative levers and a panel of on/off switches. Plus instrumentation. But this ship was different. Lots of input and output. Setting registers all over the place. A profusion of dials, a sensor hood that looked like a beehive, a set of spinal electrodes. Some people like to fly a ship as if they were undergoing a major operation, but not me. Some people like every imaginable data available to them on the panel, like how fast is their heart beating, and how much ash is there in the ashtray. But I want to know what's vital and what's necessary, in that order, and nothing else. At that point I was sure that I couldn't fly the ship and never would be able to. Nor anyone else, for that matter.

"It takes some getting used to," said delArco. "But most

of the monitor devices are on automatic circuitry. You don't have to worry about the spinal hookup, because that all works without any conscious control. The hood's so big because of the vastly increased sensory range and sensitivity made possible by the organo-metallic synapses in the ship's nerve-net. You can achieve a much higher degree of integration with the ship than you ever could with a conventional model, and this will make the sheer complexity of the controls less frightening. It will take some getting used to, but once you're acclimatized, the directness of sensation will more than compensate for the profusion of incoming and outgoing signals. You can be the ship's *mind*, literally—its reason and its judgment. You'll be more a part of this ship than you ever could be on board your old *Javelin*. The *Hooded Swan* and her pilot are inseparable. They are the same super-organism. You can be a *giant*, Grainger—a spacefaring giant."

All of which, if it were anywhere near true, added up to an incentive which no spaceman could possibly ignore, slavery or no slavery. If delArco was right, what he had to offer was well worth selling my soul for. But he who hesitates is rarely lost, provided that he spends his hesitation in constructive thought.

I hesitated.

VIII

"I'm not a fool, Grainger," said delArco. I had my doubts. The shipbuilder was a stubborn man, and he didn't really know what he was about. He was an Earthsider, not a spaceman.

"I'll be the captain of the *Swan*," he continued. "But I'm not going to tell you how to fly her. Nor am I going to try to tell you what's impossible and what's not. All that anybody requires of you is that you do what you can."

"But if at any time you tell me to do something and I don't, *for whatever reason*, you could have that twenty thousand back on my neck before I could turn around."

"The situation won't arise," he persisted. "I'll be on board. So will Johnny. And the engineer they're sending out from New Alexandria. And maybe Eve as well. I'm not going to tell you to drive us through a star. This ship is precious. Not just in terms of the money that's gone into her, but in terms of making a point, of proving her worth. We could all make a fortune out of her if we handle her right, and New Alexandria will have established the positive value of their integrative work with the alien races. This could bring all the peoples of the galaxy closer together."

I laughed at the last comment. "Don't try to make out you're pouring your sweat and blood into it for the ultimate good of interstellar understanding," I said. "All you want out of it is the money. And what do I care about that? I'm on a two-year contract for damn all. Count me entirely out of the financial interest."

"We'll make your fortune too," delArco promised. "Stick with us and when your two-year contract is up we'll make a new one."

"Pull the other one," I said. "It lets loose the dogs of war. What the hell use is a pilot once the ship's proven? I'm a short-term investment, and I don't even get danger money."

"You get twenty bloody thousand, and that isn't cheap for a pilot."

I sighed. But he was right. I might not see the cash myself, but there was a lot of it.

"OK," I said, about to give way. "Just one more thing. Exactly where do you intend taking her on her maiden voyage? How are we going to show her off to the unsuspecting stars?"

DelArco grinned like a wolf. "I intend to make use of existing resources, where publicity is concerned. I'm going to preempt the Caradoc Company's big scheme and steal the *Lost Star* from beneath its nose."

"You're going to *what?*"

His face fell slightly. "I thought you'd like the idea," he said. "You owe Caradoc a slap in the eye."

"Have you ever been *near* the Halcyon Drift?" I asked him.

"Not exactly."

"Is this your idea, or did you dream it up because you thought I'd like it?"

"The instructions came from New Alexandria. They want the *Lost Star*. They want the publicity. They've built a ship which can live in the Drift. It all fits nicely, from their point of view."

"Lovely," I agreed. "But have you considered it from *your* point of view? You have an unproven ship. An unknown quantity. She's never even flown out of the atmosphere. And you want to take her chasing wild geese in the filthiest mess that you can think of. I'd want to have been sitting at those controls for half a lifetime before I'd contemplate going anywhere *near* a dark nebula."

"We haven't got half a lifetime," he retorted. "Caradoc won't keep their circus going forever. If we want to steal their thunder we have to steal it soon."

I threw up my arms. "You're a shipbuilder, delArco,"

I complained. "You must have enough sense to realize that you simply can't do things this way. It's just not a sound proposition. It's far too dangerous, and so bloody *pointless.*"

DelArco was through arguing. He'd had enough. I tend to get on people's nerves, if I argue with them long enough. "Look," he said. "You now know what we're going to do, when and how. You know the terms of the agreement. I've said all I can say. Why don't you just go away and think it over. If you want the job, let me know before the end of the week. You can have a further ten days to learn the ship before we lift for Hallsthammer. And that's it. As simple as can be."

I turned abruptly on my heel and walked out of the tower, out of the yard. I was thinking: It can't be done. Not now, not ever. I've been in the Halcyon Drift and I'm never going back. *Never.*

—You sound like a coward, the wind threw at me. You've been searching at every step for a new excuse not to get back behind the controls of a ship. That two years on the rock has turned you back into a little boy. You've lost your nerve, Grainger. You've lost everything.

I didn't spare him a thought.

Cool evening air hit me and turned the sweat on my face icy cold. I wiped it away. My cheeks were burning, but a few deep breaths calmed me down. My heart slowed too.

A languorous, gloomy dusk was settling over the ship-yards. The towers seemed to grow into the gathering darkness. The very faint sound of distant metal clinking on metal in the still air, echoing even further away.

I began to walk, not caring about direction.

—Forget it, advised the whisper. You're just playacting.

Go to hell, I said.

—Do you think somebody's going to follow you? The girl, perhaps? More melodrama. Which fool are you going to play this time? More hard sarcasm. More I don't need any help. More I owe you all a grudge. Or are you going to change the tune? Play I'm afraid. Play I just can't take it. Why don't you just for once be honest with yourself. You want this job. You need this job as badly as you ever needed anything. You're not afraid of the Drift, nor of the ship. You're afraid that *you can't do it.* That's all.

Leave me alone.

—I can't do that. You're not alone now and you never will be again. You have to learn to live with me, even if you can manage to keep yourself apart from everybody else. And in order to make that a lot easier, you should go back and take that job. It isn't a joyride, but you don't want a joyride. If you turn down this ship you might as well crawl into a hole and die. Even if she *won't* fly, even if the Drift beats her, you still have to be there.

I didn't turn back. I walked aimlessly on. The alien was quite right. It was cowardice, pure and simple. Not fear of deep-space, not fear of the Drift, but fear of the *opportunity.* It was the chance that I might not be up to it, the chance that I *couldn't* become the heart and the soul of the *Hooded Swan.* Cowardice.

I wandered around the yards for an hour, till it was totally dark. The only light to see by was the starlight and the lonely marker lights set in some of the towers—a mute glow feigning life where there was only oldness and decay. I made my way out of the area altogether, back into the narrow, huddled streets of the port dormitory town. It began to rain, and the water hummed and rattled on the roofs and the pathways. I kept to the dark alleys, away from the wider streets where the cars hardly ever passed by anymore.

I wanted a drink, but not in some little back street bar full of silence and gloom and resignation. I walked steadily and purposefully toward the landing area, where the big, gaudy tourist traps were. Where—even now—there would be crowds in from the ships. Where I could get just a little taste of elder days—*Fire-Eater* days and *Javelin* days. Lapthorn days. Dead days.

I was well into my seventh drink and still stone cold sober when the fight started. It was nothing to do with me. Fights are always starting in spaceports. It has something to do with tradition and the honor of the fleet. Mostly they don't finish—they just kind of evaporate. It's rare for anyone to get hurt or arrested. And the bars only use unbreakable furniture.

Anyway, I wandered over to watch. A circle had been

cleared around the middle of the room, where a couple of tables and half a dozen drinks had been upset. There were six men fighting—five against one. The crowd, in true sporting fashion, was cheering on the loner while making no move to save his head from being kicked in. Not unnaturally, the poor guy was losing.

It was Rothgar.

The first friend I'd seen in two years.

Somebody knocked him in my direction. I caught him neatly by the shoulders, pinned his arms and whirled around so fast the others never saw where he went. The circle folded in tightly around me, and my back hid Rothgar from his assailants. The five men peered myopically around, slowly dropping their hands as they realized that they were no longer under attack. Knowing Rothgar, I was in no doubt that it was they and not he who had been attacked.

He squirmed, and twisted his head to look over his shoulder into my face. He didn't recognize me, and tried to kick me. I kicked him back.

"Rothgar, you bloody fool, it's me," I said. *"Grainger!"*

"Oh," he said. "Hi. How many did we kill?"

"None."

"How many did we knock down?"

I shook my head, and let him go.

"You're losing your touch," he said. "We should have been able to handle that lot."

"You were on your own," I said.

"Now that's what friends are for," he said. "You lousy bastard, why didn't you help me?"

"I did," I told him. "I stopped the fight."

"Bloody hell."

"You were losing," I added.

"Getting old," he excused himself. "They move too fast these days. Grow up in high gee or something."

I sat him down in a chair and looked him over. White-haired, three or four days unshaven, dark-eyed. Medium height, but still trying to look bigger than he was, and walk bigger, and talk bigger. His hot temper was cooling quickly to room temperature. He sagged a bit, and it wasn't because they'd roughed him up much. He *was* getting old. He looked a bit ridiculous, stumbling out of a fight with a false air of triviality, as if it were all in an evening's fun. It wasn't. Not anymore.

"How've you been, these last years?" I asked him.

"Ah, you know the routine. You lift on anything with a drive. You sort out the mess the last bastard left. You nurse the baby and hep her up. Then they kick you in the balls and drop you in the shit. Saved a couple of ships, maybe broke one or two up. I forget how long two years been. Maybe I told you before. They're all scared of me now. The lines don't like to touch me anymore and the companies hate my guts."

"I went down," I told him.

"That what went on? Alachakh told me you must have hit black rock. I saw him on Hannibal and we had a long talk. He had big business there. A lot of money and big noise on Khor. He's got a good ship—a big one. Still calls her the *Hymnia*, though, like his first ship. Not good for her, that—giving a new baby a dead ship's name. I told him but aliens don't always understand a thing like that. And Alachakh is a big man, since I don't know when. He doesn't take much notice anymore. He's old, you know."

Being old is serious for a Khormon.

"You know where Alachakh is now?" I asked.

"Out at the carnival. Hallsthammer."

"Carnival?"

"Drift dredging is the new fashion. *Everybody* is doing it. Lots of dumb kids flocking around the Caradoc boys. All the old hands figure if the kids can do it, they can do it better. The Halcyon is sure crowded. I heard tell of a couple dead when I came in. But nobody's anywhere near the jackpot yet."

Alachakh in the Halcyon Drift? That didn't seem to make much sense. Alachakh was no idiot, and he wasn't spacedrunk either. Only old. But even if his time was coming, he *wouldn't* take it in the Drift.

"Is nothing happening in the whole damn universe except the search for the *Lost Star?*" I complained.

"Nothing that anybody cares about," said Rothgar. "People don't care much anymore. Times have changed."

"I haven't been away *that* long," I muttered. Nobody cared much anyway.

"Ach," said Rothgar, expressing intoxicated disgust, "it's only a circus. Been going on too long. Time's running out. Only a month or three left in it. Then they'll leave the poor old *Lost Star* lost forever. Shouldn't have called a ship by a name like that. Aliens again, I'll bet, or rich men, or women. Nobody should call a ship lost before she lifts. What do they expect from her? Still, if we all go digging for her, maybe she won't be lost after all."

Suspicion invaded my mind.

"You're not, by any chance, in from New Alexandria to ride a ship called the *Hooded Swan?*"

"Sure," he replied. "Only New Alexandria will hire me these days. Only people got any faith in a man's hands. Everybody else wants the instruction book to do the flying. They offered me a good job."

"Drift dredging," I said flatly.

"Sure," he said again. *"Everybody's* doing it."

And how many men would "everybody" contribute to the Halcyon's already considerable total of victims? But did I care? Did I care if it was Rothgar, or Alachakh, or Caradoc's thirty ramrods, or Johnny Socoro, or Eve Lapthorn? Or me?

"Fate," I said, "has it in for me. It has doomed me to fly that ship. I am condemned by circumstances to fly into the core of the Halcyon, to play chicken with time-schisms and lesions and all other breeds of perverted, mutilated space. Everywhere I turn I meet the Drift. What the hell else can I do?"

"I lost you," Rothgar complained.

"It's nothing," I said. "Just that when I came back from Lapthorn's Grave, the Drift came with me. It's riding on my back, and I can't shake it no matter where I go."

Rothgar didn't bother complaining again. He just assumed that I was drunk.

I sat back in my chair to think. It wasn't coincidence, of course. The links between delArco and Eve Lapthorn, between New Alexandria and me, between my brand of flying and the ship—all these had existed before. But someone had gone to a certain amount of trouble to weave a web around these links from which I couldn't escape. The New Alexandrians, of course. Computermen all. Devious minds. They liked things nice and orderly. They liked to set things up. And they had. They'd be just now checking their answers with a slide rule.

I'd always liked the New Alexandrians, while I'd worked for them before. But now I was building up a little bit of resentment. What got me most of all was that I didn't believe that I was worth the trouble.

"You want another drink?" asked Rothgar. "I got paid."

"Fine," I said. He got up to go to the bar, then turned back to face me.

"You the pilot on the *Hooded Swan*?" he asked.

"Yes," I said, resigned to my fate.

He grinned. "It'll be good to fly with you," he said. "I like a pilot who knows what he can do. Out on the rim they say you're the best. I say it too, which is maybe what keeps the story moving. You know how it is."

"I know," I said. "I say the same about you. Maybe we talked ourselves into a job we can't do."

He laughed. "They shouldn't have called the ship that name," he said. "But it's not so bad as all that. We can live through it."

Then we got drunk.

IX

Johnny woke me up the next morning, dragged me into a sitting position, and shoved a cup of coffee into my hand.

"What's the matter?" I wanted to know. "I wasn't that drunk. I'm perfectly all right."

"Eve's downstairs," he said.

I started to groan, but thought better of it.

"What does she want?" I asked, in neutral tones.

"You. I can't imagine why."

"Don't you start," I said.

"Don't you ever stop?" he retorted. I gathered that he was annoyed about something.

"I made myself a little unpopular yesterday," I guessed.

"You were a little tiring," he said.

So much for my attempt to raise a few obvious objections and submit them for rational discussion. DelArco obviously had Johnny on his side. Which was understandable. The kid had never been in space. I drained the coffee cup and gave it back to him. "Cold," I commented.

"You're welcome," he said.

I got dressed at an unnecessarily leisurely pace, and then wandered downstairs. Eve was seated. Johnny leaned against the wall, eyeing her covertly.

"Let's go for a walk," she said.

"What for?"

"Because I want to talk to you."

"Not about that bloody ship?"

"Not directly," she said. "I want to ask you about Michael."

I nodded. Johnny looked a little less than happy as I eased past him to the door, but I turned in the doorway to shrug helplessly at him. He returned the gesture.

The sun was shining brightly but wetly. Dark clouds were still drifting to the north, and the pavements were still wet with the rain that had lasted all night. We wandered in the vague direction of the Northeast Area. This side of New York Port wasn't a great place for strolling but Eve had something on her mind—real or imaginary—and she wasn't paying any heed at all to the shabbiness of our surroundings.

"The world where Michael was killed," she said. "It was on the edge of the Halcyon Drift."

"Not far inside the fringe," I said.

"Why were you in the Drift?" She wasn't beating around the bush. I saw what she was driving at right away.

"I told you," I said. "We were making a run for Hallsthammer from Adadict looking for some cargo."

"You weren't going to try to locate the *Lost Star?*"

"No, we weren't."

"Where were you going to take the cargo you picked up on Hallsthammer?"

I shrugged. "Around. Depends mostly on what it was. Probably tried to pick up some cloth and suchlike for a world named Rosroc. There was stuff on Rosroc we could run to Hallsthammer, if we could trade for it."

"So you intended to be around the Drift for some time?"

"Not too far away, I guess. Your brother liked it out there. But being near the Drift and being in the Drift are two very different propositions."

"I read over Michael's last few letters last night. He mentioned the *Lost Star*. Twice. Once from Hallsthammer and once before you made the first landfall out on the rim near the Halcyon. Whose idea was it, to go out there?"

I groaned inwardly. The suspicion had crossed my mind before, but I had never seriously imagined that Lapthorn might have his eye on the *Lost Star* treasure. Not even Lapthorn . . .

"Michael's," I answered her.

"Does that matter to you?"

"Does *what* matter?"

"The fact that Michael died because he wanted to go after the *Lost Star*."

"You think I ought to rush straight out there and die with him, trying the same crazy trick," I suggested. "From motives of loyalty? Or just plain sentiment?"

"But he did intend to try?"

"He might have. He acted like an idiot, at times. But he didn't say anything to me. I thought we were there to run cargo, the way we always did. That's how we made our living. I would never have let him talk me into Drift-diving. I'd never take a ship of mine into a place like that."

"But it wasn't just your ship, was it? It was his as well."

"It wouldn't fly without me. Or without him, for that matter. Wherever we went, we had to *agree* to go. I would no more let him go treasure-hunting in a dark nebula than he'd let me get a job running mail from Penaflor to New Rome. We always compromised."

"You didn't compromise at the end, did you?"

"What's that supposed to imply?"

"I know a little bit about spaceships," she said. "I've been around them quite a lot. Your ship was two-ended, right? Controls in the nose and engine in the belly."

"So?"

"So whichever end came down first would take the brunt of the crash."

"And . . ."

"The man at the controls might have no chance of avoiding the crash, but he might have plenty of time to change the attitude of the ship."

"I told you all about the crash," I said. "I didn't kill your brother deliberately."

"You could have flipped that ship. You had the time."

"I was spending the time trying to get us down in one piece. I didn't make up my mind before we hit that one of us was going to die. I was fighting an all-or-none battle. I was trying to save the ship, and stop her from smashing us all into little pieces." But it wasn't as simple as that and I must have known it at the time. Could I, *if I had thought about it*, have flipped the ship and saved Lapthorn's life while forfeiting my own?

The simple fact was that I *hadn't* thought about it. I'd just done what I'd done, without hesitation, by sheer reflex. It had never occurred to me that there was any choice to be made.

We'd both stopped walking. Other people were on the street, ostensibly paying us no attention whatsoever, but close enough to hear us.

"I suppose I could have flipped the ship," I said, very quietly. "I had the time."

"But you didn't."

"I didn't." Still very quiet.

"And what right had you to decide that it was Michael who was going to die, and not you?" Her voice was intense, but not angry or hysterical.

"Right?" I said hoarsely. "What has *right* got to do with it? I had the controls. If there was a decision it was mine to make. I did what I did and I never even *saw* a decision. Right and wrong don't enter into it. I was at the controls. I tried not to crash. I crashed. If the only thing in my mind had been giving your brother a better chance of surviving, then *perhaps* I could have saved him. But it wasn't. There was nothing in my mind about saving anything except the whole lot—ship and contents. *My ship* was going down. I was thinking about *her."*

"I see," she said, in normal tones. "All right."

"All right!" She'd lost me. My voice rose, helpless before her inconstant attitude. "You force me to admit that I could have engineered your brother's survival—or at least that I didn't do all I could to save his bloody life. You make out that you believe I should have been the one who was killed, and that you think I should think so too. And now all you can say is, 'I see. All right.' "

She'd started walking along in the middle of my spiel, and I was half a pace behind throughout the second half.

"I was just curious," she said, offhand.

"Oh, bloody marvelous," I said. "Thanks a lot. And now, I suppose you want to start helping me again." I felt slightly uncomfortable as I came out with the last remark. "That reminds me," I added.

"What did it remind you of?" She sounded slightly surprised.

"I owe you an apology."

"What for?"

"I thought you put delArco on to me. I sort of blamed his first visit on you."

"I told him where to find you."

"Yes, but it was the New Alexandrians who were so keen on his hiring me. I thought he was acting on your say-so. He did say that his backers sent him, but I didn't really believe him."

"I shouldn't worry too much about it," she said.

I decided that I was entitled to a little curiosity as well.

"Exactly what *is* your part in all this?" I said. "What are you doing on the crew of the *Hooded Swan?*"

She hesitated. "I'm the monitor for New Alexandria. They're recording the whole trip on a shipboard device that records sensory impressions. They'll be recording history using my eyes."

It didn't sound right, somehow. I wondered whether there was any reason she could have for lying. While I was wondering, I somehow forgot to ask exactly what sort of job she had with the delArco organization.

"Are we still short of a pilot?" she asked me.

"No," I said. "You're got your hired hand."

She looked pleased, as if she thought she'd talked me into it.

X

Three days later, I thought I was familiar enough with the controls to lift the ship. DelArco wanted me to do so, right there and then, but I was more cautious. I wanted to work the controls on the ground—inside the tower. I think delArco was offended by the calculated deliberation of my schedule. He was in a hell of a hurry to commit suicide.

The captain couldn't seem to understand that while I sat in the control cradle, hooked up and doing absolutely nothing, I was working hard. I was doing *necessary* work, too—just acclimatizing to the sensory range and potential of the ship, just feeling the size and the shape of my new body. DelArco knew every relay in those controls, all right. He knew what every inch of wire was for. But he didn't understand *how* to use it.

I had to have the contacts in my neck resculptured in order to fit the spinal electrodes comfortably. It's hell to fly with an itch where you can't scratch, or with a clip that pinches even slightly. I insisted on having the hood modified as well so that it was perfectly tailored to the shape of my skull, the distance between my foveae, the depth of my face. All this took time that delArco thought was dead. He seemed to believe that all I had to do in order to learn the ship was to take her on a joyride to Pluto and back. I wondered long and hard why the New Alexandrians had made him captain of the vessel. It was a job he simply wasn't fitted for. He was a screwdriver and bank-balance man, not a spacer.

Only Eve seemed to understand the process of getting

74

into the ship's skin—and she was the only one I could stand to have in the cabin during most of the time I spent there. But I still didn't manage to fathom out exactly why she was on board, except that it was connected with a vague idea she had about following in her brother's footsteps. I didn't know whether she was trying to follow his example and escape from her claustrophobic home life by the same route, or whether she was on some kind of pilgrimage to try to justify his existence. Lapthorn was dead, but he was still hanging around. He was riding inside Eve just as the wind was riding inside me.

Four days before our scheduled lift, delArco hit flat panic. He practically tore the hood from my head in order to get my attention.

"They've got it," he said. "They've collated all their mapping data and they've found her. They know where the *Lost Star* went down."

"So what?" I said.

"So we have to move! They'll reach her as soon as possible."

"That's right," I agreed. "Approximately three months, if they start from Hallsthammer."

"They're in the Drift already! One of them might be practically on top of her."

"No chance," I said flatly. "The *Lost Star* is in the core. The ramrods are outside the core. They wouldn't go in there just to poke around. There's a big difference between the velocities you can maintain in the corpus of the Drift, and those you have to keep to in the heart. They haven't a cat's chance of getting within spitting distance for weeks. Mapping the Drift worlds is difficult enough, thanks to the distortion. Reaching them is a problem of an entirely different order. Don't worry, Captain, we have all the time in the world to finish the game and beat them too, provided that this bird lives up to the advertising material."

He didn't like it, but I wasn't breaking my schedule for the sake of pandering to his raw nerves.

I didn't actually take her up till the day before our official lift. She had to be moved anyway, from the tower to the takeoff bay. The port authority didn't take kindly to having the full power of a ship's cannons released over the shipyards.

I decided to stay inside atmosphere, and just put the ship through some elementary procedures. There was nothing that hadn't been done while she was test-flying, but it was the feel that was important this time. I could get some idea of what she'd actually do while we were en route for Hallsthammer.

It was sacrilege, of course, to use a ship like that for creeping about at thirty thousand feet and a thousand miles an hour. But you have to learn to crawl before you can attempt to stand up on your hind legs and howl.

Despite all the hours I'd spent sitting at the console with everything switched on, the first time I put the hood on for real it felt completely different. The sensors were beautiful—tuned and focussed exactly. Through the ship's thousand eyes I watched the tower split, and the halves roll back out of our way. I put my hands around the levers, and felt the power growing inside them, swelling up from the bowels of the ship.

For the first time, I began to get some positive sensation in my ship-body. I could feel the wind that blew across the yards. I could feel threads of force reaching out from the gathering drive to the limits of the nerve-net. I felt the *Hooded Swan* come alive inside me. My heartbeat fused with the rhythmic discharge inside the piledriver. The flux-field of the mass-relaxation web was cold and inert, but I could sense its enfolding presence, like a carefully clutching hand. And the background sensation—the knowledge that I was the ship, the admission of common identity—grew stronger.

The dials whose information was reflected in the hood around the image of the empty sky showed the gain creeping up to the meager potential that was all I could use in taking off from the yards.

"Count me down," I told Rothgar, and he began calling off the last few seconds. As he reached zero, I tensed, and the whole ship with me. The cannons began to burn, with no real power. The reaction in the thrust chamber swelled calmly, and we rose from the ground in the arms of the blast.

Lazily, the massive hull heaved herself from the ground, standing on the cannon-fire, balancing with utmost ease, climbing up and up and up. I was holding her back right from the start, cradling her as she was cradling me, holding her gently like a great big baby, balancing her, blowing her over feather-light, into horizontal flight, buoyed up by the air and not by her own power. I let her soar for a moment or two, and then pushed her into our predetermined path.

The wings carved the air like great knives. I counted seconds until the first turn, and then I eased myself into the nerve-net, curling my left wing and turning to the right. With a calm, fluid sweep of my fingers, I brought us back again, smooth as silk and feeling as natural as if I'd been born a bird. The thrill of the wind was all over my arms and along my spine and under my belly and between my legs.

The *Hooded Swan* was a bird. She could fly. I took her -high, furled my wings, and dived. I swept her around and around and around, and out into straight flight again.

And then we went home. I was flying myself—high as a kite on my own adrenalin. I practically floated her down to the bay where she was scheduled to spend the night. There was a crowd on the port watching us. Either the HV had been tipped off about our clearance to lift, or they were very quick off the mark. A lot of people had drifted in from the port connurbation to watch us drop. They didn't see much. A drop is a drop. Things *fall* down. A lift is something else again. I wondered how many of them would be back at six tomorrow morning to wave good-bye.

Once I'd burned off the high and got a chance to relax again, I began to add up the score. On the surface, everything had been perfect. I had the feel, and I knew now that I could fly her. But was it the right feel? The test flight was a sham, in a way, because atmosphere makes a big difference to the performance of any ship. Anything could do aerobatics under the conditions I'd used. Supercee maneuvers were a completely different matter. I'd proved nothing, except that it felt good to be inside her hood.

Rothgar came up from the depths, and we congratulated each other silently. Eve and delArco left to make preparations for lift. I didn't envy their task of coping with inquisitive sightseers.

"Everything OK?" I asked Rothgar.

"How do I know?" he replied. "The deration field is the

key to the drive, not the thrust chamber. Until we use the flux we won't know for sure whether she works or not."

"But nothing's wrong?"

"Of course nothing's wrong. Would I allow anything to go wrong? She will do whatever she can." Rothgar turned, and went back to his glory hole.

I turned my attention to the slightly uneasy Johnny Socoro.

"Don't you have any work to do?" I asked him.

"I have to check the cannons from outside," he replied. "But not while that crowd's still hanging around."

"DelArco will get them cleared away," I said. "He'll give the port authority hell for letting them in, in the first place."

"Can't keep them off the port," Johnny pointed out.

"A little effort would keep them out of this bloody bay. It could be sealed, if the authority could be bothered. Legally, they're trespassers."

"Does it matter so much?"

I shrugged. "Not to me. It's delArco's ship." There was a pause. "Well," I continued. "You got what you wanted, didn't you? Shipping out from Earth in the morning. The Halcyon rim in a couple of days."

"I don't know why they hired me," he said. "I've no experience in space, and I'm not too familiar with this type of drive."

"Maybe they were in a hurry," I said. "I shouldn't worry too much about it. If they had any specific reason, then it was in the interests of neatness. The New Alexandrians are neat people. The pilot of the ship is a key man, and they probably planned to build the crew around me. All that's really new in this ship is in my job, so they could afford to pass up the best men for the other jobs in the interests of giving me people I know and can work with."

"Then why is delArco captain, not you?"

That had been bothering me, too. I had to tell him that I simply didn't know. But I had my suspicions. While delArco was captain, I was nothing. A ship's captain has a great deal of responsibility, and hence a certain amount of authority under the law. A captain can exercise discretion about where to take his ship, how and when. Maybe the New Alexandrians only wanted my talent, not my ideas about how things should be run. While I had no power in the eyes of the law, they had complete power over me by virtue of their contract.

Johnny left to help Rothgar check out the drive. I had work to do as well—laborious checking of every circuit I'd used, to see that everything was still working as it should. But for the moment, I wanted a couple of hours rest. The flight had left me exhausted. So I leaned back in the cradle and talked to the wind.

You got your way, too, didn't you?

That was the first time that I ever initiated conversation with the wind. I was getting used to him, and accepting his presence as something more than just an unpleasant fact that I couldn't do anything about.

—I got *your* way, he replied.

It's nice to know someone has my interests at heart.

—I have both our interests at heart. So should you. They ought to be more or less the same. A dispute could prove embarrassing.

Maybe so, I agreed, then added: But more so for you than for me. I have the casting vote, don't I? I own the body.

This was a point which bothered me—just what was the wind capable of, once he was settled in? Could I be dispossessed of my own body?

But he agreed readily enough that I had the body, and in the event of a dispute, he'd have to go where I took him. I reflected that if I were he, I would object most strongly to being taken into the Halcyon Drift.

XI

The second takeoff wasn't much like the first. The day before, I'd choked the life out of the piledriver before it had any chance to develop real thrust. This time, it was all for real—the cannons would really let go, and the flux would flow.

I held her on the pad while I poured impulse from the discharge points into the deration system, to cycle the flux and build up a syndromatic power charge that would hurl us clear of the Earth within seconds after I let her go.

The bird climbed on the blast as if she'd been lusting for clear space all her young life, and now it was offered to her, she couldn't wait to grab it. I threw the relaxation web into operation the moment I closed the cannons, and a surge of power spread through the nerve-net like a shock-wave. Suddenly, the whole subsurface was alive and participating in the thrust. The bird was really going now—not lifting on the cannon-blast or soaring on her wings, but *driving* on the internal release and consumption of power. She was living.

Faster and faster and faster.

I couldn't see the Earth in the hood, save as a location mark. Even the sun was dwindling visibly into a forlorn point of light.

"Countdown to tachyonic transfer," I told Rothgar calmly. I always sound calm during takeoff. He began in the two hundreds, which meant that I was anticipating slightly —a fraction overanxious. I spared a second or two to pull myself into perfect concentration. I ignored the count till it was down below eighty, accelerating smoothly and gathering more power in the web, bleeding thrust out of the driver into the flux and preparing to flood it back. The relaxation field began to grow around the thrust, balancing out the mass-gain.

Rothgar was holding the plasm in absolute balance. It flowed as smooth as a great river, despite the load it was carrying. I caressed the load with my fingertips, feeling its readiness to respond to the slightest pressure. I eased her gently into the line which delArco and I had plotted as a course. She slotted neatly into the groove without the slightest bleeding from the flux-field. Most ships had trouble grooving—they lost power and time, and occasionally damaged their shields in the matter-dense outer-system space. But the *Hooded Swan* moved with the grace of perfection.

The count reached twenty and I had time and power in hand. She was clean and even—no delay in reaction, nothing she couldn't do. No force, no persuasion—the ship was myself and we acted as a whole. We were one.

As the count dropped to single figures, the relaxation field grew taut and began to strain. The loaded flux wanted to break and jab, but Rothgar and I had it between our fingers, and it kept flowing. I had thrust in my right hand, deration-plasm in my left. I had to keep the balance perfectly, as well as holding the groove. Approaching the Einstein barrier, whether from subcee or transcee, the balancing equation became more and more difficult. The tachyonic transfer from one to the other had to approach instantaneity as nearly as was possible. If I overdid the thrust, the flux-field would blow, and all the plasm would bleed out of the system. If I overextenuated the piledriver we'd fail the transfer and lose the load from the flux. Either way, we'd have to start all over again.

But the count reached zero and I didn't even have to think. Just reflex and feel. The load swelled back into the piledriver and the impulse hurled us across the barrier without a phase-flicker. She was stable during every instant. The plasm held her perfectly. Immediately, I calmed the deration field right down. The thrust grew in my hand as I took the restraint from the impulse. In tachyonic reverse, the velocity climbed exponentially as I denatured our effective mass. I eased off at five thou, and let her coast at constant. She was still sitting in the groove, and we were in clean space.

I leaned back, and closed my eyes.

"She'll move a lot faster than that," I heard delArco say, as if from a great distance. I was tempted to invert the gravity field and hope he didn't have the clasps in his chair fastened.

"Not now, she won't," I told him. "She'll do as she's told."

He said nothing more. I detached the hood carefully, pulling away the contacts from the base of my neck. I unclasped, but I didn't leave the cradle. Real pilots never do, while their ship's in space—only liner jockeys.

"Somebody get me a cup of coffee," I said.

There seemed to be a certain amount of confusion about who was doubling as steward. The finger finished up pointing at Johnny. Eve, for the moment, at least, did not consider that a woman's space-place was in the kitchen.

I surveyed the instruments directly with a critical eye, but everything was as it should be.

"Well?" said delArco.

I paused a moment before replying. "OK for now," I said finally.

He'd been expecting praise for his ship, but doing without wouldn't injure his pride too much. I wasn't going to rush into enthusiasm regarding her performance and potential.

Once we were well clear of the solar system, I got down to the serious business of finding out what the *Hooded Swan* was capable of doing in deep-space. I increased velocity gradually, cradling the thrust control in my hand and waiting for Rothgar to complain, or for the flux-field to waver and threaten to lose its integrity. The further I damped the relaxation web, the more delicate the required manipulation would become. The resistance to the control lever was geared, but there were only a hundred and fifty degrees to move it through, and the gearing was inadequate once we were over twelve thou. After that the only limit was the delicacy of my handling. She was up to forty-seven-thou—and I still thought I had her well under control—when the warnings began to come through. The field was beginning to evaporate. I brought her back to thirty thou and rested. Rothgar never said a word. Apparently, he could balance the flux at any velocity. The limit was defined solely by the continuity of the field, which was determined by the design of the drive. She was faster by a factor of ten than any other mass-relaxation ship I'd ever heard of.

DelArco, seeing that I was resting at the controls again, came over to scrutinize the instruments.

"Get out," I said. "And keep your mouth shut." He moved away without saying anything.

"Is everything all right?" Eve asked him, whispering in an effort not to disturb me. He must have nodded in reply, because he said nothing and she lapsed into silence again.

I slowed down again to twenty thou, paused for thought and then decided not to be ambitious. I took her down to ten.

"It's playtime," I said. "Sit down, clasp in, and if you feel the need you can worry a bit. The gravity field will be the first thing affected by any strain, so don't panic if down becomes sideways."

I waited until the sounds of their clasping in subsided, and then I returned my attention to the hood.

"Ready, Rothgar?" I said.

"Sure."

"Now listen carefully." I spoke with exaggerated clarity into the microphone. "I'm going to take the ship out of the groove in a slow arc. Then I'm going to tighten the curve until we're moving around the groove. If we jerk, tumble, or spin, I want you to flood the plasm with all the power you can get. Keep it moving at all costs—I don't care how much thrust we lose, so long as the field stays intact. The moment there's trouble I'll take us into a tangent. Right?"

"Got that," he replied.

"OK. I'm going to load the piledriver and hold the discharge, so the power will be there when it's needed. We're off."

I paused again, mustering my courage as well as my concentration. What I was about to do would be impossible in any other ship. Maybe in this one too.

I pushed power into the piledriver and held it there, not

letting it flow into the nerve-net. I scanned the instruments inside the hood, then let my eyes drift out to focus on the circle of dim starlight which was all I could see in a tunnel of darkness.

I let my tactile senses spread via the electrode contacts until I was sure that I could feel every synapse in the vessel. I couldn't feel them as entities, but I could feel the wholeness of the system.

My hands grew into great wings, my spine was the ship's long axis, my legs were the tail stabilizers, my groin the atomic cannons, my heart the relaxation web wrapped around the drive, my lungs the ship's lacunae.

I waited and waited until I was absolutely sure that my identity suffused the ship and vice versa.

Then, with an assurance built on little except arrogance, and faith in the perfect feel of the ship, I brought the ship away from the deadline along which she was traveling.

I flew. I flexed my wings to use the strength that was in them, curled them to channel and direct that strength. I kicked slightly with my legs, and my spinal muscles rippled inside me.

My heart leaped, but instantly, its surge of panic was stilled and contained as my hand palmed the lever. For just an instant, the systole seemed to hesitate as the flux reached a stress-point, a moment of decision. But Rothgar was riding the drive, and the flux ran calm and safe. The relaxation field was steady and firm. The internal gravity field was still and firm.

We climbed and we circled and we fell and we zoomed in a gigantic arc. Slowly, almost languidly, I began to tighten the arc, to reduce the radius of the spiral. My body bent and my wings billowed, and I could feel in the tenure of my bones and the texture of my skin and the tonus of my muscles *exactly* how much she could take. I *knew* beyond all doubt what my ship could do, because I was she and she was me. *My* ship, was the *Hooded Swan*. Mine.

I could fly faster than light.

I could fly higher than the stars.

I could fly through clouds and through rainbows.

I choked.

A hand of cold metal clasped my throat with a grip that

was not too tight, but icy cold, and froze the breath in my throat.

The *Hooded Swan* cried out in pain, and I heard the voice of my own scream rattling off the walls of the control room in jagged echoes, with Eve's scream answering it in resonant anguish.

I fought for air, my panicked wings beat briefly, and we came out of the arc on a tangent. The bird soothed her ruffled feathers, and Rothgar, down in her womb with the drive, caressed his child back to life and sanity.

We were clear, and sliding back feather-light into the comforting slot that was our programmed course. I breathed deeply, still feeling the pain that had possessed my throat when the flux jammed. There were great red bruises on my neck—so Johnny told me afterwards. I felt for and with my ship. Her pain was mine, and her injuries were mine. If the *Hooded Swan* were ever to go down, I need not worry about spending another two lonely years on some bleak rock.

The silence lasted a long time. No one else moved until I had the hood off my head, and was rubbing my neck and my face with both hands. I wiped my face with my sleeve, and was relieved to see that what came off me was all sweat and no blood. But I think I was worried more for the bird than for myself.

"What happened?" asked delArco.

"Nothing serious. The flux in the relaxation web jammed. The plasm distorted. But it was only momentary. Rothgar flushed out the trouble with the power we held in reserve. She took it easily. She'll take it again, if need be. You're right, Captain. Your ship will turn at transcee. She'll maneuver in deep-space. She might even take us in and out of the Halcyon core."

"When you screamed," said Johnny, "I thought we'd gone."

I shook my head. "It was surprise more than hurt. I didn't expect it to *feel* like that, inside me instead of around or underneath me. I *knew* it would, I guess, but knowing it isn't the same as taking it. It was a false alarm. The *Swan* barely whimpered."

"Is she all right?" demanded delArco.

"Perfectly," I assured him. "The operation was a success. The patient is in good health. She'll do what you say."

"And in the Drift?"

"I'll answer that in the Drift. For now, I'll push her back to twenty thou, and then I want a rest. And some food."

I could sense words hovering around behind me, unsaid. Captain delArco or no Captain delArco, I ruled the control room. Which was as it should be.

XII

We made almost dead level time to Hallsthammer, once I'd worked out an ETA based on what I knew the ship could do and what I wanted to do with her. It took nearer three days than two, which annoyed delArco, but whatever was burning him up wasn't my affair. I was in no tearing hurry. The *Swan* had done all that she was asked to, and looked casual while she did it, except for that one momentary indiscretion while I was pushing her a little too hard.

There was no crowd in the bay to watch us land—a fact which surprised me until I found out how many cops it took to keep them away.

"Whose is the private army?" I asked delArço.

"The port's, of course," he replied.

"And who's looking after the drunks?"

"The backers requisitioned all the police support they thought we might need. They care a lot more about their ship than the New York Port Authority."

"They're here, then?"

"Of course they're here. Didn't you suppose they'd want to know how their ship flies, and to have a look at their crew?"

"Very understandable," I said. "Why didn't we fly her to New Alexandria before coming here?"

"Time," he said—not for the first time—"is of the essence."

Personally, I'd have forgiven Caradoc anything if they'd lifted the treasure of the *Lost Star* that very evening, and saved us the bother of killing ourselves. But delArco was determined that we should make a race of it, win by half the length of the course, and collect the prize and the glory. It's easy to have ambition when your part in the action consists of sitting around and inquiring after other people's health.

"Do we stay aboard and wait for them?" Eve asked.

"I'm going ashore," Rothgar stated bluntly. "Grainger and me, we stink." He looked sideways at delArco, who'd hardly sweated a drop all trip.

"We'll see them at the hotel," said delArco. "We'll have dinner in their suite."

"Oh Jesus!" commented Rothgar. I didn't like the idea either. This was delArco's job, not mine. He was the builder—the moneymaker. He maybe owed the backers a fancy suit of clothes and a nightful of pretty talking. All I owed them was a pair of hands wrapped around the controls. Rothgar too. Eve, of course, saw nothing wrong with the plan, and Johnny seemed ready to tackle it manfully. I foresaw a great deal of discomfort and embarrassment all around, and I said so. But the captain put his foot down, and exerted his authority. I might be the driver while we were upstairs, but he wasn't going to let me call the tune while we were on civilized soil. He was the lawfully appointed boss.

Rothgar told him that he was several exotic varieties of a lousy bastard—maybe hoping to be confined to quarters —but delArco just ignored him.

While preparing to face the dinner, I had the temerity to doubt the intelligence of the New Alexandrians, whose idea it probably was. Later, I realized that maybe they weren't stupid after all—just crazy. They knew we wouldn't like it, and that's partly why they did it. When we walked through the door of their suite, Rothgar practically broke out into a rash. I wondered how long it would take him to lose patience and start stirring his tea with his fingers—just for effect.

There were three New Alexandrians, and delArco introduced them proudly to the assembled ranks of his crew. One of them I'd seen before—a white-haired, wizened old man with eyes as bright as a bird's. His name was Titus Charlot, and I'd known him while Lapthorn and I were working as entrepreneurs extraordinary for the Library.

The other two were younger, and looked more like big money than big brains. New Alexandria has her passengers like everywhere else. They have intellectual standards which are rigidly maintained, but there's no Law of New Rome that says a man with intelligence has to use it. And people who have money as well quite often get out of the habit. Silas Alcador and Jacob Zimmer were their names.

They all knew Eve already, and they greeted the rest of us with all the ersatz pleasure which the salubrious surroundings demanded.

Dinner was exactly as farcical as I expected. It also seemed well-nigh endless. But eventually, by sheer necessity, the party broke up and relieved us all of the hideous attempt at togetherness. DelArco closeted himself with Alcador and Zimmer to discuss practical details of the *Lost Star* search, and to give them a full account of our journey from Earth to Hallsthammer. Rothgar elected to get quietly drunk while pretending to pay attention to this conversation, supporting his pretense with the occasional semi-relevant snide remark. Johnny prowled around in Eve Lapthorn's wake until she was forced to talk to him in order not to have him perpetually leaning over her shoulder. She couldn't muster the unkindness to chase him away.

Titus Charlot picked on me.

"Vile, isn't it?" he remarked, with unconvincing friendliness.

"It's your party," I reminded him.

He shook his head. "I don't like this kind of thing any more than you do. But it's the way men like Silas and Jacob conduct their business with men like Captain del-Arco. We are dragged in against our will to complete their idea of a full picture."

"I thought *you* were the boss," I said, a fraction sharply.

"Not at all," he replied silkily. "My concern is principally that of the scholar. I led the team which processed and integrated the Human and Khormon corpora of knowledge and thought. Silas and Jacob are concerned more with the financing and material handling of one or two of the projects resulting from the synthesis. We are merely allied. I have no authority over them."

I was nearly a foot taller than Titus Charlot, yet he seemed to be looking down on me. And talking down to me as well. It was suddenly borne in upon me that this man practically owned me, lock, stock, and barrel, and that he knew it. And that he was pleased by it. It occurred to me that Charlot didn't like me, and I couldn't quite see why.

"It's a long time since we last met, Grainger," he said evenly.

"Not so long," I said. "I've a few friends I haven't seen in longer."

"You haven't got any friends," he said coolly.

"Not here, apparently."

"We remember you, on New Alexandria," he said. "We always thought very well of the work you did for us. The value of what we eventually gleaned from what you brought us was priceless—immeasurable in terms of money, of course, though I imagine we underpaid you shamefully. When I heard that you'd been picked up I was delighted to have the opportunity of repaying you. I'm very happy to have been able to help you." His voice was dead flat, and he was practically drooling false piety. He was putting a great deal of effort into making sure that I understood that he didn't mean a word of it. I found the overacting more insulting than the intention. But I couldn't fathom out what he had against me.

"Who told you I'd been picked up?" I asked suddenly, wondering if it could possibly have been Axel Cyran.

"News travels fast," he said. "And all news goes via New Alexandria. We like to know everything."

"I don't suppose," I said airily, "that you exercised any sort of influence on the court which handed me the ticket for twenty thousand? Just so you could offer to buy it back?"

"Of course not," Charlot replied. "I'm surprised you should imagine that a court on New Rome could be influenced in any way. The New Romans are very jealous of their proven honesty and integrity."

"Yeah," I said, to show that I didn't believe him.

"Let's not spend too much time being expressively clever. It's a great strain at my age. Tell me what you think of my ship."

A lot of people seemed to think of that ship as their own personal property. In legal terms, Alcador and Zimmer must own it, and they were the only ones I hâdn't heard advancing a claim. I saw things this way: What Charlot had owned was a big computer and the pickings of other men's minds. What Alcador and Zimmer had owned was a stack of ready cash. What delArco had owned was a metal and plastic scrapyard. The *ship* didn't really come into existence until she flew. And in deep-space, she was all mine. She *was* me. Ergo, she was my ship.

In telling Charlot how she behaved and how she handled, I spared no effort in conveying this point of view to him. He didn't like it.

"You can't understand," he sneered. "She's all mine and only mine. History will give her to me."

"That's true," I conceded. "But then, they write the history on New Alexandria, don't they? And by the time the *Hooded Swan* is history, I won't care too much."

"This goes a lot further than your meager existence, Grainger," he assured me. "You're only a very tiny part— a tiny *mechanical* part. The ship is mine, Grainger, and so are *you*. I couldn't fly the ship myself, *so I bought a machine which could*. That's you. No one else is important. Alcador, Zimmer, and delArco are just the hired hands. Eve Lapthorn is nobody, and that extra crewman too. Rothgar is just a transient. He won't last long enough to register his presence."

"You mean you set this whole thing up so that you could claim all of the credit? Is that all?" I laughed at him. It wasn't funny, but I thought amusement was called for.

"That's right," he said, with sudden intensity. "*Credit*. Not to claim it, but to feel it. I want what's mine, and I don't intend to let any of it go. But it's not credit for a fancy spaceship that I want. Not *only* that. The *Hooded Swan* is only a very small beginning. It's the beginning of what the Human race came out into space *for*. It's the fusion of alien science with our own. It's five hundred years of conceptual development in a single stride. It's the result of a perspective gained from two different points of view. The universe is by no means a simple place. The real nature and potential of matter and time and force are millions of years beyond our crude brains. We have to develop, to evolve, in order to have any hope of ever understanding the universe in which we live. The *Hooded*

Swan is only five hundred years worth of groping in the dark, of advancing along the chosen path of our narrow little minds. But it's a beginning. Not just of new opportunities in star-travel, or new sensations for spacemen.

"It's the beginning of a new kind of evolution. From now on, evolution isn't a matter of selection by elimination of the weakest— you have no idea how *crude* and *inefficient* that is! From now on, evolution will come about via the *fusion* of the strongest. It will comprise the *growing together* of all the intellectual races. On New Alexandria we will integrate every race into a coherent pattern of summed knowledge, philosophy, attitude, intellect, creativity, potential. We will form a cohesive, corporate supermind. From that supermind will come the potential for a new environment—not just new technology, but new ways of thought, new ways of life. Once the supermind exists, the environment can advance to meet it. Once the environment begins to change, all of the races will adapt to fit it. Our supermind will begin in our computers, and in our few fortunate selves. But it will expand to encompass *everyone*. All men of all races. To any man will be available the knowledge, the philosophy, the aesthetic capacities, the emotional capacities of *all* men, whatever their race. And from the synergistic integration will emerge *new* knowledge, *new* understanding, *new* appreciation.

"Together, Human and Khormon can know and feel more than they ever could if they had remained separate. All the races together will come to know the universe as it is. We will become universal beings. We will possess a universal mind.

"The fools who originally wanted the human race to come out into space thought in terms of its *conquest*. They were so stupidly ambitious as to imagine that the scum of one tiny planet could own the universe. Intelligent men have a different idea. We want to *be* the universe. We want to achieve our full potential within it—we want to achieve identity with it. And we can. The fusion of Human with Khormon hasn't *doubled* our knowledge. Far more than that. It has created whole new fields of thought— directions which our poor simple brains never realized the existence of. The two become a greater one by far than the sum of its parts. And when we have added everything

of all the other races into the supermind, we will have a
one of such tremendous potential that it is beyond our
trivial imagination.

"From this moment, evolution at the intellectual level
no longer divides and diversifies. It *unites*. We have a goal,
and we can attain it.

"You, Grainger, are an ephemeral. And a mindless
ephemeral at that. You *can't* understand. None of this belongs to you. Only to me. This is what I have begun. This
is the credit that I want."

He stopped, and steadied. The intensity drained out of
him.

I just couldn't say anything to him. Nothing at all. To
myself, I said that he was insane. That he was a real, genuine, authentic mad scientist.

—He means it, said the wind.

Oh sure. He means it. He's got the grandest delusions
of grandeur in the galaxy.

—You've got a sterile mind, said the wind. Can't you
understand what he says? Can't you appreciate what he
wants?

To hell with his fancy dreams, I replied. That's just so
much junk. I don't give a damn for superminds and the
harmonization of human and alien thought. That's just
froth—empty air. What I care about is what it's making
him do to *me*—to the ship and all who sail in her. I don't
care how philosophically elegant or aesthetically appealing
his spiel might be. I don't care if you fall in love with his
stupid dreams. I care about my life and the fact that he
doesn't. He owns me, remember. He bought me because
he needed me, and he couldn't afford to let me have ideas
of my own. *That's* what scares me. *That's* his madness.

—You have a very dull mind, Grainger, said the wind.
Constantly preoccupied with trivial matters. You have no
soul.

With that parting sally, the wind retired gracefully into
implacable silence.

Meanwhile, back with the mindless ephemera, delArco
was bidding his fond farewells. This task was made no
easier by virtue of the fact that he and Johnny were supporting Rothgar, who appeared suddenly to have become
too heavy for his legs, and who was muttering angrily to

himself. Eve was fluttering around them like a helpless moth, getting in their way.

I retreated, leaving dignified thanks floating behind me. I helped the others support Rothgar, and we descended in the elevator.

"Did you know," I remarked conversationally, "that our employer is completely and utterly mad?"

"I know," said delArco.

I was astonished by his perspicacity. "So why do you work for him?"

"Because he pays me. He's not harmful or dangerous. He just has some strange—and rather quaint—notions. Our business is flying a ship. I don't see how the two are incompatible." I canceled the re-evaluation of his perspicacity. He was still an idiot.

"Sometimes," I said, "I have the feeling that fate is not on my side. Not only that, but it also has a grudge against me."

DelArco laughed briefly. "It's you that has the grudge," he said.

—Amen, added the wind.

XIII

The next morning I slept.

During the afternoon, delArco had to go see Charlot to collate some information and try to establish a sensible basis for our attempt on the *Lost Star*. Johnny and Rothgar were refluxing the drive, but I had nothing at all to do —there was no point in trying to make up some sort of excuse for a flight plan. You can't make plans to deal with the likes of the Halcyon Drift.

I took the opportunity to relax for a while—it was the last chance I'd get for a week or more. In the evening, I met Eve for a drink in the port's showpiece—a high tower with a bubble of glass set on top from which tourists could get a great view of the Drift. You also got a great view of the squalid area back of the central port where the locals conducted whatever trivial business had brought them to the rim. Much more to my liking was the vast expanse of the spacefield which stretched for ten or twelve miles away to the south, ribboned with truckways and pockmarked with private hangars and bay gantries. The *Hooded Swan* was a long way off, closeted by high fencing and protected by booms slung across the approaches. But she was a tall ship, and I knew her well enough to visualize her lines and compare her to the ranks of ramrods, dirt-trackers and p-shifters which were parked closer to the tower. The other mass-relaxers dwarfed her with their massive, six- or eight-shielded hulls, but they were just big and ugly. She was more or less of a size with the lighter p-shifters and the bigger yachts, and she looked a little uncomfortable compared to their silky, polished skins. But I knew how frail and false that mirror-brightness was.

I let my eyes dwell on the alien ships, all shapes and sizes of them, which were scattered all over the tarpol. They were mostly the dimensional hoppers of free traders, but there were a few dead slow dredgers which made their living on extended jaunts into the quieter parts of the Drift, trawling the sleeping dust-clouds and sorting out anything of any value—ore, organics, gemstones, anamorphosed matter. They wholesaled their collections maybe twice a year on Hallsthammer. It wasn't much of a living, considering the dangers inherent in the Drift work, but it kept the ships flying and the crews fed. A lot of spacers asked little more than that, though humans as a rule are either too ambitious or too quarrelsome. We are basically a vain and aggressive people.

I searched briefly for Alachakh's *Hymnia*, but remembered that he now used the name on a different ship, and that I wouldn't recognize her.

Eve looked at the sky, not at the ships. Her fascinated stare betrayed the fact that she hadn't been in space more than a few days. Even casual tourists are careful to lose the open expression of cosmic astonishment as soon as they can. Nobody likes to be labeled a dirt-grubber in a galactic age.

Hallsthammer's sun is a weak red giant which never cleared the horizon in these latitudes by more than a handspan or so. The northern sky was always ruddy with halflight, sprinkled with a few luminous clouds. The tangled mass of the Drift lurked higher, crouching behind the red haze like a vast, crippled spider suspended on a tenuous web of starlight.

The Drift is technically a dark nebula, because of its occluding clouds of dust—in the inner wheel, people see it as a dark blot obscuring the stars behind it. But it contains a good number of stars within its body which retain visible magnitudes on Hallsthammer and a few neighbor worlds. So the dark nebula is quite bright and beautiful—if you like that sort of thing—at close range. The light is refracted and distorted by the nebular corpus, and it shines all kinds of colors, and changes its face constantly. Even at high noon it has an angry, sullen glow which rivals the sunlight. The perennial ebb and flow of its contortive currents make it hard to look at for long—the star-storms are always blasting matter back and forth in time, and from the light-dense core to the thin shell, and sparks flare and die all the time, each one burning a blur into your sight.

"It looks terrible," she said. "Like a great hand with crippled fingers that keep clutching and coiling."

"That's what it feels like too," I told her. "Fingers always plucking at your skin, poking into your shields. A constant rain of dust and radiation. It fumbles ships to pieces like a child pulling apart a crane fly while trying to hold it still."

"And yet they give it a name which suggests a more pleasant disposition," she commented, her lips forming the word "Halcyon" as though she were tasting its softness.

"Rothgar's theory of names," I said. "Appease the dragons, make love to the ships, insult dead worlds, and compliment live ones."

"How very poetic," purred a new voice, from behind us.

"Alachakh!" I said, turning quickly and reaching out to touch him. We gripped hands hard, and placed our free hands on each other's shoulders. "I hoped you'd find me," I said. "I asked about you, but no one knew who you were at the port. You know how it is. You look very prosperous."

He plucked modestly at his clothing, which was expensively cut and perfectly proportioned, not spacer stuff at all.

"They force it upon me," he explained. "They like to deal with men who look like themselves. I have not your pride. I bow to them and they make me a rich man." He was being polite. Alachakh was a proud man—he had a great deal to be proud of. The Khor-monsa were smaller, on average, than the human race, but Alachakh was a remarkable physical specimen, and matched my height, although he was far from my weight. He *looked* burly, his sleek skin stood a long way from his bones, but his flesh was far less dense than human flesh.

The Khormon face is flat, the olfactory organ pushed back into a slit-like cavity and the eyes tilted in an odd manner. Perhaps the oddest feature—by human standards —is the string of sonic receptors circling the skull like a headband—small, rigid plates suspended at various angles

in a flexible neuronic membrane. Khormons are far more
sensitive to vibrations over a far wider scale than humans.
But the Khormon is also far more vulnerable to physical
attack by virtue of the sensory apparatus conferring this
ability. A Khormon skull is extraordinarily amenable to
fracture. By necessity, they are a peaceful people. They
are proud of their peacefulness and their friendliness. Their
mingling of statutory pride and hypocritical politeness
leads the men of many other races to profess distaste for
their ways and their persons. Personally, I like the Khor-
monsa. But then, I do not like humans.

I introduced Alachakh to Eve Lapthorn.

"I knew your brother very well," he told her. "I was
very sorry to hear of his death. I was very happy at the
same time, though, when I learned that you"—he addressed himself to me now, of course—"had survived and
been returned to civilization." His voice was very quiet,
and whirred softly. His native language consisted of little
more than constant whirring, but such was the sensitivity
of Khormon sound orientation that he could reproduce
almost any native language with perfect fluency. He had
made it his business to learn at least a dozen languages—
three of them human—for the purposes of politeness. The
fact that the Khor-monsa are the great linguists of the galaxy was no doubt the crucial fact determining that they
should combine with the New Alexandrians in the pilot
project in the integration of racial identities.

"Rothgar told me that you have a new ship," I said.

"And you too," he said. "A ship we have talked about
for some time here on Hallsthamer. She has a reputation
already."

"Part of the credit belongs to the Khor-monsa," I told
him. "You know about the scheme of which she is a part?"

"I know. But I am too old to appreciate the grandness
of the plan. To me, she is only a ship. I am entrenched in
the past, and I cannot look to the future as you might."
His manner was sober, and I knew that this was a matter
of great import. Khormons do not fade away into old age
and declining health. They have recognizable limits, and
they know them well.

"I wonder that there are no Khor-monsa involved in the

building and operation of the ship," I said. "It would seem a logical thing to do."

Alachakh shrugged. "Human jealousy," he explained. "Earth is a world split into factions. You people thrive on the mistrust which breeds possessiveness and trading sense. A human is unwilling to treat anyone except his closest friend as an equal, and he harbors doubts even about his friend. Your ship is a human ship, my friend, not a Khormon ship."

Alachakh would never have said anything of that kind to any other man but me. I was surprised that he said it where Eve Lapthorn could overhear, if she wished. I don't know whether he assumed that she was still engrossed in contemplation of the sky, or whether he was becoming tainted by long association with humankind. After all, he seemed suddenly to have acquired a great deal of trading sense of his own.

"Which is your new ship?' I asked him.

He glanced out of the window. "I can see her," he said, "but she is too far away to see clearly. She is over there, but I doubt that you can be sure which ship I am pointing to. The port is unusually crowded these days." He was right. I couldn't pick out his ship.

"Very crowded," I echoed his words as we turned away from the window and sat down at a nearby table. He ordered another round of drinks, and Eve came to join us when they appeared.

"Exactly what are the crowds for?" I asked. "Surely they aren't all Caradoc ships."

"The Caradoc ships are in the deep Drift," he replied. "They know where their prey lies, and they are hunting her with lunatic ruthlessness. She is in the core, of course —almost certainly within a transfigured domain, embedded in a lesion. Their maps of the Drift are good, but nothing can be perfect where nothing is stable. They move slowly by necessity."

"I heard that you might be in the Drift with them," I said.

"I would be," he replied, "but for one thing."

"One thing?"

"You, my friend. I wanted to see you."

"Sentiment?" I asked him, slightly sarcastically. He shook his head.

"To make a deal," he said. "A trade. You are taking your ship after the *Lost Star*."

"Not by choice," I assured him.

"Nor I," he said quietly. "And that is why I must try to beat you to the target. You have a wonderful ship, so the story is told. She will go in and come back again. I have a good ship. She will go in, fast enough to beat the company, but she will not come out again. Do you see what I mean?"

"You're getting old," I said. "So is Cuvio. This job is important to you."

He nodded. "If you will allow me to lead you into the Drift, then I will guide you to the *Lost Star*. If I cannot reach her, she is yours. If I do, then she is mine for one day. Then you can take her. I will not be coming back. The glory will all be yours."

"How do you know where she is?" I asked.

He sighed. "The power of money. I have been unfortunate enough to become rich, and the rich have access to many secrets—they have aged me quickly, cluttering my mind with useless embarrassments. I bought this particular secret from a Caradoc captain. Some others have done the same. I have no doubt that your employers could buy it if they wished. But it might take time. They might not buy it in time. The *Hymnia* will fly faster than any ship has ever flown in the Drift. You won't catch me. You might as well come with me."

"They won't like it," I told him.

"But you can make them accept it." He smiled. "And you will, my friend, won't you? You don't like the terms of your contract. That fatal pride, my friend, it makes you predictable."

I smiled back, without much humor. He was dead right —I'd take every opportunity I got to set myself up against Charlot and delArco. Also, Alachakh was my friend. If he needed to reach the *Lost Star* so badly that he was going to kill himself doing it, then he must have a powerful reason. I didn't have any reason at all for finding the wreck. Even if it was stuffed full of treasure, it wouldn't be my treasure. I'd far rather Alachakh reached the *Lost Star* than I did.

"We'll do things your way," I assured him. "But I don't see why."

"I grow old," he said again. "It is not so easy, as one grows old, to move about one's mind. One falls prey to fixations. It is easy to become obsessed. One's aims become separated from one's judgment. The walls are sealed tight in one's mind. The doors no longer open. I often envy you humans, who can live all of your life in one constant stream, with all your identity and personality simultaneously present. It would be well worth forgetting a few trivia in exchange for mental unity. But you are the great traders of the galaxy. You have the good end of the deal. Ironic, is it not, that humans are united within and divided without, whereas the Khor-monsa are exactly the other way about?"

"You're not so old that you've become deadlocked," I said. "You don't talk like a deadlocked man. You can still reach all the rooms of your mind. You haven't begun to lose yourself."

"You don't know what it's like," he told me. "I can move from room to room. Slowly, and with effort. But they are all so cramped, so full. Claustrophobic. There is no space in which to move, let alone expand myself. My potential is all used up. I am filled with too many secrets, too many memories, too many dreams. I never thought that I would regret that I dreamed so much, but I do. Dreams are very wasteful of the mind, my friend.

"I am a Khormon, and when the Khor-monsa are full, then they have reached their end. I wish I could forget a little and create some space, but I cannot. I am stuck in the day before yesterday. There can be no question of a long tomorrow, and I doubt the latter hours of today. Soon even the minutes will become painful to squeeze away into tight corners. One last gesture is all that I can spare. One last plan, one last goal, one last journey. I'd like to do the impossible just once more. Especially this kind of impossible."

"But why the *Lost Star*?" I wanted to know. "And why now? You could have had her to yourself at any time during the last forty years. Is it just because she's the new center of attention?"

"No. The death of a Khormon is not a matter of

fashion. I don't like to die alone. I will be glad that you are behind me. But the rest is all irrelevant. It is just that for forty years there was no reason to go after the *Lost Star*. Now there is."

"You know what she carried?" I said, astonished.

"Not precisely. I have my suspicions. But I can't tell you about it. Not yet. Not until I know that I will fail, and that the cargo will be yours. I might be wrong. There might be no cargo at all."

"You think the cargo was Khormon," I persisted.

"No," he replied. "The *Lost Star* never went to Khor. If there is a cargo, it's from somewhere that doesn't even exist." He smiled. "From Myastrid."

He rose to leave, and I rose with him, gripping his hand again. It was light and curiously intangible.

"I will see you again," he promised.

"I hope so."

"Cuvio will make arrangements for our flight. We will lift early in the morning."

He walked away, and I settled back into my chair. Eve was staring at me. "What's the matter?" I asked. "Wondering whether I just sold out your boss to the little green men? Traitor to the cause of Titus Charlot, or something?"

She ignored the nastiness. "What's Myastrid?" she asked.

"I don't know," I told her. "Anglicized form of a Khormon word. Maybe the name for a world. Have to ask an English-speaking Khormon, I suppose."

"You didn't ask Alachakh."

"He didn't want me to ask."

"What did he mean earlier," she asked, "when he talked about being unable to change his mind? I couldn't follow that."

"Khormons have sectioned brains," I explained. "They have eidetic memories—they never forget. They sort and classify their memories, and hold them in separate memory-banks—what Alachakh called rooms. Their consciousness can scan one section at a time. Their minds exist in all the rooms, but as the rooms fill up, their minds become compressed smaller and smaller. Eventually, the mind has to split, to lose its coherence. That's deadlocking. As a matter of principle—of politeness to their fellows—the Khormons usually choose to die before they reach this stage, or before the condition becomes acute. As a matter of pride, they like to perform some useful action in dying. Every Khormon wants to be a dead hero."

"So Alachakh's attempt on the *Lost Star* is a kind of ritual suicide?"

I shrugged. "Just about. I would have figured him for a less ostentatious way out. But the last two years seem to have left a big mark on him. He's not quite the man I used to know."

"You don't seem sad," she said hesitatingly. "If that man was your friend, and he just told you that he was going to die in a matter of days . . ."

"I'm not sad," I said simply. "Neither was he."

"But he was an alien." She spoke without thinking.

"So he's entitled to be polite. He's entitled to be reconciled to his death. But I'm not, am I? Not according to you. I have to put up a show. I have to cry, like they do in the movies, like they train their children to do. Well, I'd rather be a Khormon kind of hypocrite than a human one. I'll not weep for Alachakh."

"You didn't even say good-bye," she accused.

"It wasn't necessary," I told her. "Not yet. He knows I'll be there when he dies. We'll say good-bye then."

She shook her head, and refused to understand.

XIV

As Eve and I left the building, we paused reflexively on the pavement to feel the cool air. Eve looked up at the darkening sky, and my eyes flicked right and left along the street, then came to rest dead opposite, where an alien in a spacesuit was watching me. He was standing stock still, and his face was hidden inside the helmet, but I sensed from his attitude that he was staring at me, and that he was recognizing me. Then he moved his hand to his belt. I got suddenly very scared as I realized what was coming. I barged Eve to the ground, and turned to run to my right. I was acutely aware of the time the motion took, but things seemed to move more normally once I was in full flight. The gun in the alien's hand followed me, tracking the course of my run, and fired. I ducked, but I'd have been too late if he'd fired straight. The beam splashed the wall a few inches behind me. I got showered in brick dust, but it didn't hurt.

The silver-suited figure never had time for a second attempt. He was shot down by someone standing in the hotel doorway. The police had arrived with uncommon and remarkable alacrity.

I stopped sweating and walked slowly back. The cop was already helping Eve to her feet.

"Thanks," I said, recovering her from his arms. We all went across the street to inspect the cadaver.

"That's OK," replied the gum-chewing cop laconically, as he strode proudly up to his kill like a hunter-tourist. "It's what I'm paid for."

"You came out of that doorway in one hell of a hurry," I said. "Were you watching him? Or us?"

"We protect the citizens," he said.

"And today you have to protect us."

"Seems so," he agreed. "Maybe somebody knew you were going to need help. Came in that New Alexandrian bird, didn't you? Going to steal Caradoc's gold." He pushed at the spacesuit with his boot, and turned the corpse onto its back.

"Crocolid," he said, in his slow, idle tone. "We got three dome colonies on this continent. They don't often come out, with having to suit up and all. Some of them work in the port, though—odd jobs, mostly."

"Odd jobs is right," I confirmed.

"He was waiting for us," said Eve, finding it a little hard to believe. She'd led a sheltered life. Mind you, I hadn't exactly made a habit of being shot at.

"Apparently," I said, "Caradoc thought I got off too lightly on New Rome. Or maybe they thought I was being ungrateful coming back to the Drift so soon. Either way, they thought I needed a lesson." I crouched down beside the cop, who was calmly desuiting the dead alien. "Any chance of finding out who paid his wages?"

"What do you think?" he replied scornfully.

"I think the one thing I'd like to know more than anything else is whether he was paid to hit me, or whether he was told to miss," I said.

"Brother, if I were you, I'd worry," he said confidently. I couldn't quite see why anyone should want me dead enough to hire a hit man. It didn't make sense, no matter how much Caradoc didn't like me. How loudly, I wondered, had Charlot bragged about the prowess of the *Hooded Swan*? How much time did Caradoc think they needed to buy in order to beat us to the *Lost Star*?

There was a crowd gathering.

"Can we go?" I asked. "Or do we need the shadow of the law lurking in our wake?"

"I'll come with you," he said. "The wagon just turned the corner. We can leave justice in the hands of the almighty."

He was discreet about following us back to the ship. He turned away every time I looked back over my shoulder.

I was glad to get away from the port again. Maybe Hallsthammer is a bitch of a world where people get gunned down in the streets every day of the year. I'd been on worlds like that before. But I'd never been important enough to shoot. Only a little guy with his own business to mind and no talent for stepping on other people's toes. I didn't like being important enough to be a target.

The whole affair put me in a violent frame of mind. As we passed beneath the *Swan* prior to climbing into her belly, I realized for the first time that this kind of ship could revolutionize space combat as well as space exploration. Space battles had been fought half a hundred times in the past, but casualties were so light it was hardly worth the bother. It's difficult to hit anything out in all that emptiness. But the *Hooded Swan* could maneuver. She could get in close no matter what velocity she was traveling. If she were armed, she'd be a phenominally successful warship. Maybe more than the Caradoc Company had a right to be afraid of her. Though the idea of New Alexandria as a military power was ridiculous, the idea of an Earth fleet trying to reinforce the mother planet's influence in the galaxy was oddly plausible.

"She'd make a great hawk, if she had claws," I said to Eve, to explain my silent contemplation.

"You want to use her to hunt pigeons?" she asked.

"Worms," I said. "Giant steel worms. It isn't the sportsman coming out at last. It's the pessimist. Don't let it worry you. Let's go make some coffee and tell the children about our adventure."

Johnny was dutifully concerned about the nearness of my escape from the jaws of death, but Rothgar only used it as fuel to feed his morbid outlook on life in general and tomorrow in particular. I changed the subject, as soon as it was decently dead.

"I saw Alachakh," I told Rothgar.

"I saw Cuvio," he countered. "Gave me a special bleep for tracking him. You can hook it into the control panel and it'll plot his path in our computers."

I took the small device which he handed to me. "Damned clever, these aliens," I muttered. "By the way," I added. "Do you know what Myastrid means?"

"Yes."

I was surprised. I spat a mouthful of coffee back into my cup lest I choke on it. "Well," I said. "Tell me."

"Khormon fairyland. Silly stories, you know the type of thing."

"Not the lost planet?" I said distastefully.

"Not so far as I know," said Rothgar. "Just fairyland. Strictly for the kids."

I shrugged. "I guess Alachakh really didn't want me to know what he was about. I suppose I'll find out in due course."

"Don't you have any idea what might be on the *Lost Star* that he could want so badly?" asked Eve.

"None at all," I replied.

"I'll tell you what's on board the *Lost Star*," said Rothgar. "Khormon fairyland. Damn us all."

I nodded in half agreement.

"Whatever it is," I said, "it can't possibly be of any value now. We're a whole new universe. Eighty years is a long time. Standards have changed so radically within my working lifetime that the trade routes I started out on are totally redundant today. Price is a matter of fashion, and fashions change tremendously over the years. And never so fast as during the last century. I think we'll find something in the hold of the *Lost Star*, if we reach her. But it will be worthless."

"As long as we've got something to show for it," said Johnny. "If we find her and then can't bring anything back, it'll be a hell of a bust after all this shouting."

"That's true, I guess," I agreed. "Stunt or no stunt, we'll need a few baubles to feed the imagination of the peasantry. Just so long as they don't expect miracles."

"So we win the game even if we don't find a fortune," he said.

"First time I ever saw a kid so eager not to find a fortune," I commented.

We would no doubt have carried on the conversation in much the same halfhearted vein, but we were saved the trouble by the return of Nick delArco. He was a bit steamed up. Word had filtered back to him that some unkind person had taken a potshot at his pilot. I was quite flattered by his concern. I didn't know he cared.

He and Charlot had talked to the police, without getting

much satisfaction. Since tragedy had been averted, and a convenient corpse duly registered as part of the day's haul of evildoers, the police were well satisfied. It looked OK on their books, and to follow it any further would be wasteful of man-hours and totally unproductive. The whole thing was a dead end. All delArco had got from the police was a string of interesting facts about crocolids.

The assassin's race was a relic. In their heyday, the crocolids had colonized seven or eight worlds in the neighbor systems to their home world of Hycilla. They'd progressed slowly because they had only subcee drives. To complicate matters further, Hycilla had a peculiar atmosphere which had necessitated setting up all the colonies under domes. Hycilla had then been badly knocked about by injudicious quarreling amongst the crocolids. The planetary environment took a turn for the worst, which resulted in the eventual extinction of the indigenes. Without support from home, most of the colonies had been unable to sustain themselves. The crocolids on Hallsthammer had been among the lucky ones. But stuck in the domes, fighting poisonous atmosphere, they'd been completely unable to evolve. Their society and technology had been static for millions of years. It was possible that the crocolids were the earliest known spacefaring species, though no one could really speak for the antiquity of the Gallacellens.

When the humans and the Khor-monsa had arrived—in that order—the crocolids had shown no interest at all. Inbreeding was well on the way to completely homogenizing the genetic structure of the species, despite inter-dome eugenic conventions. The intellect and physique of the average crocolid were showing distinct signs of stagnation and deterioration. Everybody tended to look down on the crocolids as an inferior class of beings. People tend to lack sympathy for losers.

Contact had been established, of course—human vanity especially can't stand being ignored. Suited crocolids had some minor commerce with the ports, but for the most part they didn't bother anybody and nobody bothered them.

It was no good pestering the crocolids about the fact that one of their brethren had tried to gun me down, because they wouldn't give a damn, and it was nothing to do with anybody except the individual concerned. It was no good trying to tie Caradoc (or any other suspect, if any) in with the crocolid, because all crocolids were identical, even outside their monkey-suits, and Caradoc—like everyone else—had irregular but not-infrequent dealings with the aliens.

I gathered from delArco's verbose and largely irrelevant account that Charlot was unworried by the incident, and had every confidence in police protection. The captain himself didn't have that kind of serene faith in the long arm of the law. He was an Earthman, which made him something of a connoisseur of criminal activities. Nobody had shot anybody else on New Alexandria in twenty years, which might have gone a long way to explain Charlot's lack of concern. I think maybe delArco was a little bit scared as well, though he needn't have been. Caradoc would surely have the sense to realize that he was absolutely dispensable. Rothgar pointed this out, and the subsequent rise in temper made it necessary for us all to retire for the night.

Next morning, we lifted.

XV

Handling the ship in the Drift was nobody's idea of fun. This was the big test—if she could be flown *safely* in space like this, then she justified her price tag. Oddly enough, I think I was more confident at this moment than anyone else. DelArco had a lot of mouth, but he wasn't so insensitive that he didn't know that Drift-driving was dangerous. Rothgar, of course, was a born pessimist, and I'd thrown enough fear into Johnny and Eve to make them petrified of every dust-cloud. But by now I knew my ship. I knew how she felt, and I could sense what she was capable of. I hadn't said anything to the others, because it was a personal matter, but I had every confidence in the *Hooded Swan*, and in my own ability to handle her even in distorted space.

The one thing that worried me more than any other was my own concentration. Under normal circumstances, I didn't leave the control cradle, but I could rest there for long periods of time. In the Drift, it would be far more difficult to relax. There is, of course, lots of empty space in any nebular structure—everything in deep-space is ninety-nine percent emptiness, no matter how black it looks from outside. But you can't really rely on any one bit of that space staying empty while you're in it. In fact, it's far *less* likely to stay empty while you *are* in it, because you provide a sort of focus for the contortive confluence of the lesions. The movements of the Drift within itself are not simply the cartwheels which the whole universe turns—Drift space casually disobeys principles which are called laws in saner corners of the galaxy.

At the heart of the nebula is a stress-zone of colossal dimensions and apparently limitless power. The fabric of space is shredded and colloided in a pseudotemporal matrix which stretches the core into many other times—and perhaps many other spaces—than this one. Gravitic orientation follows all kinds of weird curves, and causes similar anomalies in light-paths and the distribution of matter. There are worlds in the Drift—suns and planets and moons and comets, and they behave in pretty much the same manner as worlds do anywhere else. But in distorted space, you can never be *sure.* Not of planetary conditions, of absolute motions, not even of their constancy in time.

Theoretically, the Drift-worlds offered peaceful havens where I could drop ship and enjoy the luxury of sleep and silence. But could I really relax while we were in the nebula? Probably not. And we would be five days or more within the Halcyon's boundaries. If, at anytime during that five days, my concentration gave way under the strain, it could kill us all, no matter how perfect the *Hooded Swan* might be.

The first thing we met as we advanced into Drift space was the dust. Vast clouds of dust fly before the forces which wander through the Drift. It's not particularly dangerous in itself—most ships can live in dust. Dirt-trackers and alien dredgers even mine the dust-clouds. But it's one thing to smash through a cloud, bouncing it off your shield, and quite another to fly in an unsteady rain which maintains a continuous but inconstant strain on the ship's armor. If the shield begins to flaw or erode, then power may bleed away through the wound, and the unbalancing of power inevitably leads to the unbalancing of the relaxation flux. And when the flux itself begins to bleed, you have one foot in the grave.

I retained a lot of respect for the dust, and felt it carefully with the sensors during the first hour or two that we flew through it. But my mobility seemed easily capable of coping with the common intensities of flow. Minor adjustments of my wings maintained a steady relationship between the orientation of my surfaces and the rain. After a while, compensating for the changes became a matter of routine and reflex. The pattern of my reactions was automatically programmed into the helm computers, and the ship soon learned to take some of the manipulative burden from my hands, although I maintained full vigilance.

I'd hooked Alachakh's special bleeper into our standard signaling apparatus. As the bleep came in, it put a trace onto my subsidiary screen which plotted the path which the signal source had followed. When we entered the Drift, we were about two hours behind the *Hymnia*, but we fell back a little in the early stages while I treated the Drift with more respect that Alachakh thought was necessary. I stuck to the trace without using it as a plotted groove. Alachakh had the maps, but I knew that wherever the *Hymnia* could go, the *Hooded Swan* could follow, but I couldn't put limitless trust in the trace-path. The very fact of Alachakh's passage along it would make it that much more uncertain for us, as distortion-patterns homed in on his wake.

I had to warn delArco and Eve not to speak to me when I talked. To a certain extent, commenting out loud about the situation helped my mental state. But I could do without helpful suggestions, silly questions and messages of congratulation.

"I'm going to close up a bit," I said. "There's dust blowing across me and I don't want the road breaking up."

A big cloud came billowing in—apparently from all sides. It was hot stuff blasted out from the center, reforming all around us. The patter of the dirt on my wings halted for a moment, and then broke up into chaotic fingers stabbing at all parts of the shield. I rippled my wings, but I couldn't reduce all the angles of impact. I pushed extra power into the shield, and made sure the ship's heart was beating firm and strong in case I needed even more. I was relying on the storm's being of short duration. Pushing power into the shield over an extended period of time would weaken the drive-unit. There was no possibility of refluxing or repairing until we reached Hallsthammer again, and the motor would have to be treated with respect.

The bleep changed slightly.

"She's being turned," I said, and explained: "The cloud's blow-out from the center, cross-time or through gravity holes. She's pushing me off line in order to keep the pressure on her hull even."

I let her drift, of course. You don't fight your own ship. I tried to sense which way the lines of distortion ran, in case I could use them to adjust the wings to the shape of the stress-field. I eased back the thrust, letting the burst of power flow briefly into the shield to let me flutter my wings. Then I ebbed the strength gradually out of the shield. It was like peeling off a glove. The prickling of the dust became sharper—almost painful. I explored the contours of the field that was carrying it. I thought I had the shape for a moment, but it was tenuous and I had to keep feeling it as it changed slowly. I moved to meet its demands, and then boosted the drive a little. I fed the motor nerves, and began moving my wings slowly but forcefully, creating stress of my own, integrating it into the contortive fabric of the storm. The power in the piledriver, of course, was negligible compared to the awesome power blasting the dirt out of the Halcyon core. But that was random power. It was even available for manipulation, open to persuasion. I was the first man ever to harness the power of the Drift for my own purposes.

My skin began to burn as the angle of attack of my wings shifted to let the dust strike harder upon the thin shield. There was awkward pain in my back and my groin, but I had to disregard it. Then, with a sudden pressure like a breath of wind, the cloud disgorged us smoothly and effortlessly. It took only seconds for me to regain the trace-path.

Carefully, not allowing relief to hurry me, I eased the shield back to its former strength.

I reflected that many ships might have gone through the cloud unscathed, but not without putting heavy strain on their drive-units, and certainly not anywhere near our velocity.

"We beat that one," I commented, as deadness crept into my aching back to replace the muscular pain. I stretched slightly, and sat back to flex my fingers.

But there was no relaxing.

We were beginning to close up steadily on the *Hymnia*, but Alachakh was still moving very fast. Bearing in mind that he did not have our advantages, I calculated that the

load on his drive must inevitably blow it out in a matter
of days. He was flying like a madman. Whatever reason
he had for braving the Drift, it was moving him in one
hell of a hurry.

I couldn't see Alachakh's ship, not even with the fine
sensors, because there was too much confusion in the
visual spectrum. But the instruments hooked into the bleep
measured her loud, clear, and close. Sometimes, I felt the
wave of warped space that was dissipating in her wake.
That bothered me too—if she were throwing up a wash
like that, she could be tossed like a cork if she hit a lateral
lesion. The *Swan* could take that—if I was fast enough—
but the *Hymnia* couldn't.

If only you'd ease up, I thought at him, you'd stand a
damn sight better chance of getting there. But something
was driving him hard enough that while he had clear
space, he'd use it to the limits of his tolerance. He was
going like a bat out of hell.

Minutes drained into hours, and he began to pull even
more out. I wasn't about to risk getting hurt, and I didn't
copy him, so he drew slowly away again. Then he hit a
cloud and had to slam the anchors on. The cloud was
local and narrow, and I went through it without difficulty,
needing no particular cleverness to negotiate it.

At seven hours, distortion began to force us apart.
Alachakh didn't slow down, so I supposed that the warp
was coming in on his tail. I rode the waves for a while,
but they kept pressing in on my chest and bending my
back, so I had to slow down and take things a bit easier.
Even so, a dull sensation of pain began to gather in my
intercostal muscles. I was sweating heavily, and feeling
very tired. I'd taken a shot before we lifted which should
have guaranteed me for ten or twelve hours, but I suppose
the load was unusual.

"What's the bloody fool trying to do?" I wondered. "It's
not a race. Or does he think that I'll cheat him unless he
reached the *Lost Star* with a couple of hours to spare?"
But that wasn't it. He knew I'd give him the first crack at
the wreck, just as I'd promised. If it really came to a race,
I'd win. I had a bird and he had a bullet.

More hours.

The strain got to be too great. I know as well as anyone

else the danger of hyping up too far, but I daren't go to the other extreme and risk getting too slow or even blacking out. "Get me a strong shot," I told delArco, "and rig the intravenous feed with a bottle and a half. I can't take this on the standard procedure. Not without slowing down —and I want to stay close enough to Alachakh so that trace-path holds. I don't want a lesion obliterating the space he's flying through."

The captain moved to comply.

"Are you all right?" I asked Rothgar.

"I can eat," he replied. "Johnny can take the drive while I rest."

"Take a shot," I told him. "Don't let Johnny take too much. When there's trouble, I want you on that drive to keep the flux steady. Johnny's not trained to juggle plasm."

I think it was Eve who pushed the stay-awake into my arm, but I didn't look around. I felt the needle of the feed go in as well, and the tape to hold it. I felt uncomfortably as though something had punctured the shield on the port wing, and several minutes passed before I had rid myself of that strange sensation.

Dust, dust, and more dust. We were in the dead haloplasm of the nebula now, well inside the fringes where the outblast from the center reformed. Bearing in mind what we'd already accomplished, there should be nothing here which could hurt us, unless it took me absolutely by surprise. I wondered how Alachakh kept going. The Khormonsa are not as strong physically as humans. Perhaps he had a perpetual drip rigged up with some sort of brain-booster added. I'd flown like that before now—it felt good while I was actually in the cradle, but it had taken me three days to recover from a hundred-hour flight. It's not good for the health to ride a constant high.

The crazy chase went on and on. He touched six thou several times, but mostly stayed at four to four and a half. That was plenty for me, and I didn't copy his occasional bursts. As a result, he drew away over a period of time, but lost all the ground he gained when a web of cloud forced him to a crawl. Later, he seemed to rethink part of the course he had plotted, and I closed right up on his tail while he worked out a new way of getting from some unknown point A to point B. Caradoc's mapping had held

up perfectly until then, and the fact that it had finally led
him into quicksand was no fault of theirs. Mapping the
Halcyon Drift is an essentially optimistic task.

The bad storms which Alachakh had avoided by his
course amendment were encroaching upon my field of
view to my left. A chaotic fuzz became steadily larger inside the hood. Well before it threatened to touch the ship,
its presence was hurting my eyes. Alachakh brought his
velocity up to ten thou, obviously planning on outrunning
the monster. I had no alternative but to follow him. There
were only about six or eight minutes separating the ships,
but the storms were threatening all kinds of evil. I took
the *Swan* up to eighteen thou before I was sure we'd beat
the bad weather.

The high velocity involved penalties of its own. The distortion waves coiling away from Alachakh's tail caught us
hard, and tried to turn us inside out. The bird used my
reflexes to flip the pressure aside while I debated the slim-
ness of our chances. I shouted Rothgar to full attention,
and played tricks with the thrust, hoping he could keep
the flux under a tight rein. I had to let the g-field go at one
point in order to ride a kink in the wave. If there'd been
temporal deterioration melded with the warp, we would
have lost all our flux, or been badly crippled.

As it was, we were kicked high and wide. It was like
being tossed by a bull. There was only fragmentary pain
during the seconds we were held by the warp, but the real
bang came when we were free again. We were all wrong-
way-everywhere. I felt like I was being beaten up compre-
hensively in a matter of microseconds. It took everything
I had to right the ship and get our g back.

When I'd eased back to a comfortable velocity, and re-
settled the *Swan* on Alachakh's trail, I spared the time to
apologize.

"With luck," I added, "there shouldn't be many moments as rough as that one." The hurt showed in my voice
—much to my surprise. The pain had been just a matter
of fact. I'd had to bear it, because I couldn't spare the
time to bend to it.

The pain was soon gone again, though, and things became relatively easy for a time.

The *Hymnia* began her steady gain once more. Alachakh was impatient. He wanted to reach his appointment with death early. I didn't know how much further we had to go, but our destination had to be inside the core, which meant another day or thereabouts. I tried to guess how much punishment we'd have taken if we were the *Hymnia;* it wasn't a pleasant thought. I became uncomfortably sure that Alachakh simply wasn't going to make it. He was going to die—achieving nothing—and that bleep was going to carry his last despairing cry: the coordinates of the *Lost Star* and the mapped course for getting to her.

As the time passed, I wondered if the Khormon would even spare the time to rest. He must need to stop, I thought, even to give him a chance. Whatever elixir of life is draining into his veins, he can't keep going forever. He must make a drop soon. Caradoc must have plotted the worlds if they'd mapped this channel. He must know of somewhere he could set down. I was so dead tired, I even began to think that he ought to stop for *my* sake.

And eventually, when patience had all but been strained too far, he slowed to a crawl, and fell away toward a star-system. We followed her down. I knew that even on the surface I'd be on call at every moment. But if trouble came, it would come slowly. I'd have time to wake up and run. In the Halcyon Drft, it can be a great relief simply knowing that you don't face instantaneous disintegration.

XVI

The landfall was a ball of bare rock about the size of Earth's moon. Airless and completely lifeless, completely devoid of character and identity.

The instant I closed down the drive, I called the *Hymnia*.

"Is she still in one piece?" I asked Alachakh, somewhat breathless after the release of tension.

"We fare well," he said. "And you?"

"Unscathed," I said. "But you don't fare well and I know it. How bad is the bleeding?"

"We can contain it. Cuvio and I can direct some time to revitalizing the unit, now we are down. She will fly again, and fly high. Don't worry."

"Can you make it to the core?"

"Yes, I think so. Tomorrow. There will be no more stops."

"Take it easy."

"I can't. It has to be tomorrow. Once we have landed, we can never take off."

"You *are* in bad shape, then?"

"Shape enough for our purposes, I hope. We have only one thrust to make, and we are home. You must make another drop before entering the core, or go into a tight orbit around a safe sun. I will transmit you the coordinates of the worlds which I know, and you may take your choice."

"And what will you be doing?"

"Don't worry. The trail will be clear. You can follow

118

me when you are able. But remember that you have to
come out again. Take care of yourself."

"How far is it?" I asked him.

I could almost see him smile. "Twenty-eight hours to
the core. Twelve or thirteen within. If I do not reach it,
then the signal will tell you all you *need* to know. If you
want to know more than that, you will have to come to me
when the *Hymnia* dies. I hope she will not be blasted all
over the core as thin dust."

"Good luck, Alachakh," I said.

"I hope that you do not need luck, my friend," he replied. "I hope that your ship is more reliable than luck."

I closed the circuit, and lay back in the chair for a
moment or two. I unclasped, and stretched my limbs. But
I didn't leave the cradle.

"Is anybody dead?" I asked. All four were in the control
room. They were all watching me.

"No," said delArco.

"Good."

"Will he make it?" the captain wanted to know.

"No."

He breathed a sigh of relief. He'd never liked the idea
of being beaten to the *Lost Star*. It had been all I could
do to make him comply with necessity. I felt sure that
if I'd given him the time to confer with Charlot there'd
have been trouble. I knew that Charlot would never for-
give me that usurping of his authority, but the situation
was practically a *fait accompli* by now, and it was—when
all was said and done—the only rational course of action.

"I'm going to sleep here," I said. "I need something to
clean yesterday's shots out of my system and set me up
again for the morning."

"I'll see to it," said Eve.

"Are you all right?" I asked Johnny. He nodded. I
knew that Rothgar could and would take care of himself.
"Get some deep sleep," I advised Johnny. "Take something to make sure."

Eve came over and handed me a draft of health-restorer.

"You the doctor as well?" I asked her. "The captain's
supposed to be the guy with the know-how."

"I've been trained in space drugs," she assured me.

"Great," I said, then added—glancing at the captain—"And suppose they also serve who only stand and wait."

"What are our chances?" asked delArco patiently.

I decided there wasn't much point in letting him worry too much. "There's nothing can stop us tomorrow except a thousand to one freak," I told him. "I can't say for sure about the core. But it shouldn't be essentially different from what we've already suffered. Just more so. I think we can handle it."

"So it's all ours," he said. There was no quality in his voice—it was dead flat. He didn't want me to think that he was displaying greed.

"That's right."

"What about Caradoc?"

I shrugged. He knew full well that Caradoc couldn't have made it yet. Ramrods are dead slow. They could be within a couple of light-years and we'd still beat them.

"Don't worry about a thing, Captain," I reassured him. "It's all easy. We'll win the game."

"You don't sound as if you want to," said Eve.

"That won't stop us either," I said. "Now get me a *light* sleeper. Something that won't hang around tomorrow morning. The stuff in the pink wrapper's what I usually use. That'll do."

She winced at the mode of reference. In actual fact, I knew perfectly well what the drug's name was, but in the training schools they teach liner jockeys to be polite to chemicals, and I always avoid school methods whenever possible.

Eve prepared the sleeper, and everyone else drifted out of the control room.

As I took the beaker from her and handed back the empty one, I asked her what she was doing on board the ship.

"I'm a member of the crew," she said.

"You said you were monitoring for Charlot. You aren't. The monitor was set up by delArco. DelArco clears it and checks it. You haven't even been near it."

"We lied to you," she said. "I'm here because I insisted."

"And why did you do that?"

"Because this is my ship, Grainger. I was the first to fly

her. I went to school on Penaflor, by the way. A school
for pilots."

I was surprised, and I wanted to laugh. But I didn't,
because at the same time I realized what it must have
meant for her to hand over a ship she had flown to someone else. Taxi driver or not, she'd felt the ship just as I had.

"Why the hell didn't you tell me?" I demanded.

"After what you said about liner jockeys? Besides which,
when we first met, you made it abundantly clear that you
didn't want to know anything about any of us. How would
you have reacted if I'd told you I was a space-pilot too?"

"I'd have laughed," I said.

"That's right," she said, mimicking my cocksure tone.
"Now drink your Mickey Finn."

If you could slam a spaceship door, she would have. I
drank my Mickey Finn.

Almost instantly—or so it seemed—somebody began
shaking me. I came to life rapidly, thinking that something
must be wrong. But the sense of urgency wasn't there.
Johnny was rousing me in a normal, unhurried fashion.

I had to stand up to ease the cramp out of my body.
I glanced at my watch. It was eight hours to the minute
since we had set down.

"Alachakh just lifted," said Johnny.

"He didn't call?"

"No."

"Just like him." I eased myself back into the cradle, but
didn't reaffix the sensory hookup or the hood.

"Get me some solid food," I said. "Got to get my gut
working properly."

"It's ready," he said. "Eve'll bring it up."

"Good," I said. "Given a year or two of practice, this
may yet turn out to be a reasonable imitation of a spaceship crew." Eve brought me the gruel, and I shoveled it
down at top speed. It's not that it tastes bad, or anything
like that, it's simply that it hasn't the character to be
worthy of any more attention. Eating in deep-space is
purely functional.

Within minutes, I'd woken up completely and felt fit
and ready to tackle the Drift. We had as much behind us
as in front of—in terms of mileage, at least. There was

nothing to fear anymore, provided that I kept my eyes open and my wits alert.

And, in fact, day two went almost exactly the same as day one. It was fast and tricky, but it never looked like flooring us. There was dirt in vast quantities—the further we went, the denser the clouds. But only dust, calm dust, which rustled softly against my wings. The distortional effects grew steadily worse, but familiarity bred sufficient confidence, and facility for my task in flying through it remained more or less at the same level of difficulty. I suppose it was easier to handle than I'd had any right to expect, but I wasn't offering any thanks to fortune. We didn't need luck. Storms we saw in plenty, but none chased us. We took a battering once, about twelve hours into the day, from bad swirling dust, which hurt me a bit as it peppered my face and burned my arms, but the strain in my mind wasn't nearly so bad, and that made up for the hardship.

Alachakh was indomitable. The *Hymnia* seemed to be taking it all in her stride. She was a fraction slower than the previous day, rarely touching five thou. It was still far above what I'd previously considered to be prudent for Drift work, but on the basis of yesterday's experiences it was practical, if not wise.

It was twenty-seven tiring hours before I decided to part company and take a break before we made our final hop. When I began to drop, the bleep gave a kind of strangled burp. I played it back through the recorder, suitably slowed down. It said: "Make good use of your time. Everything is well. I may see you again tomorrow."

I'd slowed down the bleep enough to hear the words clearly, but I'd missed absolute synchronization with the recording speed. It didn't sound like Alachakh's voice. It was fast and high. It had an almost hysterical note that couldn't have been further away from the calm, deep tone which he would have used. The important word, I knew, was "may." It was practically a guarantee that Alachakh wouldn't make it. He knew the *Hymnia* couldn't do it, but he was too polite to say so.

"That's right," I said, "Don't say good-bye yet."

I set down on the nightside of the innermost planet of one of the suns Alachakh had bleeped coordinates for during the previous night. It was as desolate as our last stopover, which pleased me. The world which is devoid of everything is the world in which you can place most trust. And when the core of the Halcyon Drift is only an hour's flight away, you need as much trust as you can muster.

I took a long look at the sky, using the ship's eyes. The core sprawled across the entire sky, filled with colored light and roiling with storms. In there, I thought, are Caradoc's thirty ramrods. And the *Lost Star*. And Alachakh. And the corpses of six or eight ships which tried to do what he—and I—are trying to do.

—Roll on tomorrow, contributed the wind, with more enthusiasm than I had. We're almost there.

This is no time for you to return to the fold, I reminded him. The fate of this ship depends exclusively on my peace of mind.

—As you wish, replied the whisper. But I'll be here. Don't forget me.

How could I?

I unclasped myself. Eve already had the pick-me-up ready. It was sharp to the taste, but sapped away all the pain and tension within minutes. When I turned to look around, delArco was busy with the monitor. "Nice collection of snapshots?" I commented. "Make sure the folks back home don't miss a thing."

He glanced briefly in my direction, vouchsafing no reply.

I called Rothgar, since he hadn't appeared, to make sure nothing was wrong. He sounded unhappy, but he assured me that the drive was in perfect health. I contemplated leaving the cradle and going to my bunk, but decided that I'd better stick to the formalities. The moment I turned my back something was bound to go wrong.

XVII

I didn't take a knockout drop, but I slept peacefully for nearly thirteen hours. When I woke up, the first thing I did was to listen for the faint, steady sound of the *Hymnia's* bleep. It was clear and bell-like.

Johnny was on watch. He turned to face me when I sat up.

"He's made it after all!" I said. "He said twelve or thirteen. He must be there by now."

Johnny shook his head. "I've been watching the trace, and he's still moving. It's been dead slow for a while now. I think it's more difficult than he anticipated."

"You can't tell that," I said. But I checked with the instruments, and he was right. Alachakh was still flying transcee. And while I sat there, peering at the trace he was making, the *Hymnia* screamed.

The ship's dying wail cut across the note of the bleep like the hopeless cry of a child. Though the bleep itself was hardly noticeable, the scream was enough to wake the dead. DelArco heard it, from his cabin. As he burst into the control room, the scream was replaced by a garbled sequence of noises. Then it cut out entirely.

"We're off," I said, sliding into the cradle and clasping up.

"Rothgar!" I bawled into the microphone. There was no answer. "Get him up!" I told Johnny. "And Eve. I want the drip rigging for feed. I can't spare the time for gruel. I'm lifting in three minutes and everybody goddamn better be ready."

"Aren't you going to play that back?" demanded delÁ-co.

"No," I retorted irritably. "I am not going to play it back. I'm going after the *Hymnia* first. The *Lost Star* can wait. If the ship's still in one piece, Alachakh still might be alive. Maybe we can give him a lift."

"Let's at least make sure . . ." he began.

"Go to hell," I told him.

"I'm here," Rothgar's voice ccame over the phone, as I adjusted the hood. "Get to work."

I got to work, ignoring delArco. If he said anything more, I didn't hear it.

I almost lifted too fast, and wobbled the g-field, but I held her and she slipped into transcee as smooth as silk. I gave her every ounce I could, and I could feel that it was too much. But it wasn't going to take me thirteen hours to reach the *Hymnia* if I could help it. I owed him five hours at least, six if I could clip the trip by that much.

Before I even realized it, we were inside the core, and I felt the not-so-tender caresses of the vast distortion fields which enfolded a globe of space many light-years in diameter.

The strain was steady, and the changing of the matrix gentle but forceful, like a tidal flow. I knew the effect on both the *Hooded Swan* and on myself would be cumulative. And the faster I flew, the faster it would accumulate. At two thou, it might take a day to cut to our heart. At four thou it might take six hours. I couldn't tell exactly how far away Alachakh was, nor what additional peril might lay in between. I decided that seven or eight hours at a steady one thou should reach her, without hurting us permanently.

Within an hour, I knew things were worse than I'd guessed.

"Ready for trouble?" I asked Rothgar.

"What kind?"

"The *Hymnia's* left one hell of a wake. It's disturbing the local field and setting up eddies. It's slowly building up to create havoc. There are time-mutilations bubbling all around us."

"No way around?"

"No way around," I confirmed. "I've got to stick to the trace or I'll never find him in this warped space. There's only one thing I can do and that's to ride on the distortion flow. It means going fast, but if I can stay *with* the current instead of cutting across it, it won't hurt us."

The one flaw to that argument, of course, was that the basic orientation of the field was crosswise to our path. We'd have to ride *inside* the storm, rendering ourselves vulnerable to its whims.

"I'm going to try to make the storm-wind blow the way we want to go," I told Rothgar. "I'm going to give the storm an eye." I licked my lips. "We've got to blast a hole behind us with the cannon and jump at seven or eight thou to avoid being blown through it. If the flux jams we'll be so much smoke. And half a million years ago at that."

"OK," said Rothgar calmly. I'd just told him to do the impossible. Like a good spacer, he didn't question the order.

"Count me down to the blast," I told him. He began the count at twenty, which was too high for my liking, but it was his drive. In the meantime, I tried to balance on the edge of the vortex that was swirling in around us.

At five I began to run. Two thou, two-fifty, three. As the count closed in on zero, I flipped her out to seven, opened the atomic cannon, and shut my eyes. Less than a second, I held the leap. I shut the cannon and closed back to three thou, holding tight and praying that I could keep her in the bounds of the known universe.

With her body contorted like a spitted fish, we writhed in agony. I was held by the clasps I couldn't yield to the tortuous demands of my muscles. I felt my spine bend and my limbs tried to flail. I knew that if a bone broke we'd be dead. The shield was all but stripped away by the jump, but I pushed just enough power in to hold it while we cartwheeled. Dust drilled into me, and I could feel blood on my arms. But the ship didn't bleed—she was strong as well as lithe, her veins were bedded deep. I could feel the power faltering, and I knew the flux was going to catch. I prayed that Rothgar could take her through the crisis. I fought for her as we climaxed, and we won. She rode the shockwave.

I'd turned the perversion of Drift-space to our advantage. It was running with us, helping us, carrying us.

"Damage?" I asked sharply.

"Don't do it again," advised Rothgar. "If you open the cannons at transcee again, you'll lose them for good."

I redirected my attention to feeling the exact strength and motion of the storm-wind. The instruments indicated my speed at one-thirty, but I reckoned, as far as reaching the *Hymnia* was concerned, we were making the best part of two thou. If conditions held, we'd be there in four hours.

Naturally enough, conditions didn't hold. They grew steadily worse as things reverted to their previous state. I had only made a *little* hole. For hours I was riding one set of waves and fighting another. I slowed down, but I was still taking punishment, and so was the ship. But the constant ache in my body was canceled by the sheer determination to go where I wanted to go. I was at war with the Drift now, and my respect for its inherent dangers was becoming a far more personal feeling—aggression, even hatred. There was an elation to be found in slashing through the cords of contorted space. There comes a stage in any battle when you forget the pain, and even the reason behind your motives. You just slog on and on, a creature of pure *direction*. I guess that having an empty, sterile, crippled mind helped me a lot just then.

It was as well that I wasn't too far away from the object of that particular thrust, because the ship might have cracked up about me while I was in that kind of a mood. There was no courage or heroism involved, any more than there was caution or patience.

To be honest, I can remember very little of what happened during that ride. I know that it took me exactly five hours and two minutes to reach the *Hymnia's* crack-up point, because the instruments later told me so. I wasn't aware of the passage of the time.

The plasm apparently clogged twice, but both times Rothgar kept the relaxation field steady and effective for the vital instants. I don't know how he did it. He was working miracles.

All in all, we were very lucky.

The *Hymnia* was drifting free—dead as could be, but still intact.

She was drifting fast on a tachyonic wind, so I couldn't

slow to subcee and call her. I had to use the drive to match her, at nearly total relaxation. I knew we couldn't sustain that for long, after what we'd already thrown away through the cannons.

I couldn't transfer from one ship to the other while we were traveling faster than light. I couldn't hang around forever hoping that she'd lose momentum, or that the wind would reverse its direction.

"I'm going to nudge her," I announced, "and take her off that wind."

That was dangerous too, but the wind itself wouldn't hurt me, and I ran no risks from dust or distortion at this velocity. Provided that I didn't injure myself fumbling with the *Hymnia,* I thought we could do it.

So I did.

Gently, I caught her wings in mine, and curled her around from the wind. I made a slightly rough tachyonic transfer, still contriving to hold her, and then I let her free again.

I got no reply when I called her. If Alachakh was alive, he was not conscious. Ditto Cuvio. The question was, could I open her up from the outside? Some people valued privacy more than safety, and it showed in the way they designed their spaceships.

I unclasped, and beckoned Eve. I sat her down in the cradle and gave her the hood.

"I have to go over there," I said. "I don't think that at this stage anything can go radically wrong. But if something comes up, she's all yours. Don't wait for me. If you pray hard enough for bad weather, you just might get your job back."

She went pale, and shook her head.

"Thanks," I said. "It's nice to feel wanted."

I grabbed Johnny as I went out.

"The lines working perfectly?"

"Of course."

"Well, I still want you in the lock. If anything goes wrong, start reeling as fast as you can."

I donned my suit, climbed into the airlock, clipped my line, and dived out. I didn't trouble to say good-bye.

XVIII

The airlock was already open. I thought for a moment that somebody might have come out, but of course that was absurd. It was open because they were expecting company. Specifically me.

I climbed in, shut the outer door and flooded the chamber with air. But I didn't take off my helmet. The ship might be holed and leaking for all I knew. There was a pressure gauge in the lock, but it was calibrated in Khormon, and I couldn't read it. I opened the inner door.

There was a corridor curling away around the waist of the ship, and a ladder leading both up and down from the metal platform on which I stood. The ship was orientated vertically rather than horizontally, as was the *Hooded Swan*. I climbed the ladder. The gravity field was still working, which was a hopeful sign. It meant that the power unit wasn't wholly dead, even if the drive had cut out. One advantage of the hopper drive was the fact that it was entirely separate from the ship's internal power circuit. Which meant that heat and light stayed on and life could be maintained. Why, then, had the bleep cut out? I wondered. Had Alachakh cut it off (in which case he must have survived the crash)? But it was more likely that the cutout had been automatic—that the bleep had been programmed to stop as soon as it had delivered its last cry and its vital message. That marked the end of its purpose—the *Hymnia's* path was recorded, its death signaled, its knowledge passed on. Old or not, Alachakh still had a tidy mind.

In the control room, Alachakh reclined in his big con-toured cradle, clasped there and looking for all the world as if he were flying the ship. But the ship was dead, and so was he.

He wasn't broken up by the climatic burst of energy which had destroyed the drive, but simply drained away with the power pile. In all likelihood, he had lived for some hours after the disaster. But I had come too late, and he had known that I would. Pinned to the instrument panel was a letter. It wasn't addressed, but I knew who it was for. For the time being, though, I ignored it.

I descended the full length of the ladder to the engine room, to make sure that Cuvio, too, was beyond all help.

The drive unit had burst, and he had been burned to a cinder by a flood of hot fuel. I shut the hatchway quickly, to seal in the heat. The radiation would be contained within the sheath of the pile. It was only the raw mass of the conversion compound which had escaped. The same thing had happened on board the *Javelin* after she went down. The scene was strongly reminiscent.

I went back up to the control room, and looked once again at Alachakh's corpse. It was taut and hard with rigor mortis. In all probability, I thought, Alachakh's death had been no more peaceful than that of his engineer. Just as the pain of the *Hooded Swan* was my pain, the suffering of the *Hymnia* had been his.

I opened the letter, and read it.

My Friend,

As you will guess, this letter was written some days ago, on Hallsthammer. I wrote it while Cuvia was de-livering the device to your ship, immediately after I spoke to you in the tower building. Now you are read-ing it, of course, I am dead. I speak these words as a dead man.

A year ago, I found a world out beyond what humans call the rim. It is a world which some of the Khor-monsa know to exist, and which others suspect to exist. It is perpetuated in our language only by the word Myastrid, which refers to what you might call "never-never-land."

It is the world from which the race now known as

Khormon originally came. The evidence exists—on Khor—but it has been suppressed, and—wherever possible—destroyed. The Khor-monsa, for the most part, believe themselves to be exactly that—men of Khor. We have told lies to all other spacefaring races. It is a small matter of pride.

I ask you not to reveal this information to any other person—of whatever race. I ask you not for my sake, but for the sake of the Khor-monsa who do not know, and those who do not wish others to know. I will not tell you where Myastrid is to be found. I hope that it will not be found. There are some of my friends there now, trying to make sure that it soon will not exist to be found. We wish to obliterate Myastrid entirely, save as a nonsense word used only by children.

We are a relic race, who now call ourselves the Khor-monsa. Our home was lost but our colony on Khor survived. We have found no trace of any other colonies, but ships are searching now, beyond the rim.

The *Lost Star* also found Myastrid. I found unmistakable traces of her in several of the dead cities—you humans are a vain people, and like to leave your mark on every world which you visit. I do not know for sure what the ship took away from Myastrid, but I am sure that the search conducted by her crew was comprehensive enough to leave them in no doubt as to the identity of the native race of Myastrid. This led to my reckless and—if you get to read this—futile attempt to reach the wreck in the Halcyon core. I did not want to steal her cargo, but to destroy it. I do not know, as I write this, how close I came to my goal.

The *Lost Star* is now yours. Her cargo belongs to you and to the others on board your ship. The secret of Myastrid is yours also. It would be impolite for me to ask you to do with the cargo as I would have done. You may need the cargo. You may stand to gain a great deal by returning it to your employers.

You have been a friend to me, Grainger, and that is why I give you what I know. I hope that you reach the *Lost Star,* because if you do not other Khormon ships will try, and other Khormon lives will be lost.

Once the *Hymnia* has failed, it is clear that no ship of ours can succeed, but that will not stop them trying. If you should feel this knowledge to be a burden, then I apologize for having inflicted it upon you.

Whatever you do, you may be sure that Alachakh agrees with you.

The coordinates which you already have will guide you to the *Lost Star.* I hope that your quest is successful.

Good-bye.

Alachakh the Myastridian.

Well now, I said to myself, what was all that in aid of? I stuck the letter into Alachakh's pocket.

I eased in front of the cradle, careful not to disturb the man inside it. I looked carefully at his controls, which were easy enough to understand more or less at a glance. I referred to his scanners, and plotted a rough course which would carry the ship into the nearest solar system, after which it could not help eventually falling into the sun. I carefully reset the controls. The *Hymnia* had no power, of course, but she had momentum to carry her. All that was needed was one short burst to realign her path. I bled the internal power to give her that burst. Afterward, she was completely dead. No light, no life. It might take her several years, but eventually she would reach her destination and her ultimate end, if the Time storms did not catch her and hurl her back into the past, or the dust-clouds shatter her as they moved on the tachyonic winds.

I evacuated the ship, to make sure that Alachakh could not rot away before he reached his burial.

Then I returned to the *Hooded Swan.*

Johnny was waiting for me at the airlock, and he helped me to take off the suit.

"Are they dead?" he asked.

"Very," I replied.

"Did you settle whatever it was you had to settle?"

"I did what I could."

We walked slowly back to the control room, where del-Arco was waiting patiently.

"All over?" the captain asked.

I nodded.

"Can we play the tape now?"

"Sure." I fiddled with the recorder with one hand, while I helped Eve out of the cradle with the other. The string of coordinates vomited out while I put the hood back on my own head, and adjusted the connections at the back of my neck.

"That tells us exactly where the *Lost Star is?*"

"It tells us what world she's on, and her approximate location. And I mean approximate. You can't get a dead fix from twenty light-years away. I'll be pleased if we hit the same continent."

"Did you find out anything else? On the Khormon ship, I mean."

"Yes. Alachakh's dead."

"Nothing else?"

"Yes. I know why he's dead."

"Why?"

"That's his business. A personal matter."

"What about Myastrid?" This from Eve.

"I didn't go over there looking for fairyland," I told her. The third degree died of starvation. Nobody was getting anyplace.

"OK," said the captain. "Let's get going. If you're quite ready."

"Aye aye, Captain, sir," I replied. I began a close scrutiny of the scanner. The printout from the computer revealed that we were very close. Poor Alachakh had gone down practically on the Lorelei's doorstep. I slipped the ship into a rough groove, and prepared for transfer.

Alachakh, I thought to myself, is bloody clever. He knew damn well he probably wouldn't make it. So he wants me to do it for him. Sure, it would be impolite to ask, but he can still drop hints like overweight anvils. He knows full well that I haven't got a reason for taking this trip—not one of my own, not a *good* reason. This trip doesn't mean a thing. Unless I use it to do a friend a favor. But if I did, Charlot would have me in jail the moment I touched soil again. Forever.

I blasted the *Hooded Swan* through the light barrier, and accelerated toward the dragon's lair.

Here we come, *Lost Star*, ready or not.

XIX

I was careful again, now that the prize was practically in the bag. I took things as easy as I could—trying to save the *Swan* from all unnecessary discomfort.

We passed close to deep lesions, and had to flutter in the grip of the distortion currents a time or two, but there was nothing new, nothing I couldn't handle with a minimum of bruising. We made the star-system in a little under three hours. But even when we were within spitting distance the trouble wasn't over. It isn't ever easy.

"There's an anamorphosis around the sun," I announced.

"What?" Rothgar's voice echoed in the phone.

"She's a focus. A doorway for the power that sweeps from the core of the Drift. A hot spot. The mouth of hell. There's a contortive domain like a cage across half the system. The fabric's stretched taut. Flying in that'll be like crawling on broken glass."

I slowed right down and drifted in, not heading straight for the star but describing an oblique orbit, looking for the exact position of the planet I wanted. The screen was blurred by the intense distortion, but I found the world without too much difficulty.

"That tears it," I said. "The bastard's inside the zone by a lousy few million miles. Of all the bloody silly places to be. I can get close at slow transcee, but if she can be reached at all, it'll have to be subcee. With no guarantees."

What made the situation even more serious was that our troubles might not end even if and when we reached the world. This wasn't one of the degenerate lumps of bad

134

rock that I'd chosen to set down on earlier. This was a genuine, honest-to-goodness planet, likely to have an atmosphere, and maybe even a life system. What might the surface be like, in the center of a distortion field like that? What sort of life forms could survive there?

"This is going to take time," I said. "And it won't be pleasant. We're going to be an hour or more inside a field which can—if we offend it in the slightest fashion—draw on a power greater than that of a thousand suns just to give a reflexive twitch. Think as small as you possibly can. This is one time in your life when you want to be absolutely negligible."

And so, having scared hell out of anyone with the sense to listen, I transferred down and commenced the approach.

Less than three minutes into it and I was scared half to death myself. I could feel that power I'd been talking about so glibly, and I'd never felt anything so colossal in my darkest dreams. It was impossible. I felt the sheer presence of the field drawing me out and pressing me in. I was draining away into my bootheels. I *knew,* as sure as I knew my name, that I couldn't make it. My hands almost fell away from the levers.

—*Move it!* howled the wind. You'll kill us all!

I gathered my melting heart, and picked up my mind in the hands of my courage. I felt the arcs of my wings and the hollow steel of my spine. I became sympathetic to the waves and the warps. I sat in the plane of the stress, and prayed that my presence there would have absolutely no effect. I found crevices in the stress, and slid the *Swan* along them, like a sleek fish moving through still water with never a single ripple.

Giant hands were around me, caressing me, stroking me, lulling me.

To kill a small mammal, like a mouse, you hold him—or her—by the tail and gently stroke the fur on his/her back with a scalpel handle. When he/she is settled down under the stroking, secure within the caress, lulled into comfort, you press down behind the head and pull the tail hard, breaking the little bastard's neck.

I felt like a mouse. But I was composed. I was very scared, but I could hold my fear. Tightly.

The deeper I went in, the worse the distortion became.

This, I thought, was *it*. The worst the Drift had to offer. Beat this and you have conquered the Halcyon Drift. You have won.

Just on and on, trying not to irritate it, trying so hard not to be noticed. Like a bedbug on a man's thigh. Like a leopard stalking. Like a hunted man in a crowd. Like the worms in my own gut.

That great big hand began to squeeze. I couldn't make it between the lines. I was running out of crevice. The pattern was too complicated. It flowed too fast. It was too sharp to feel. I was touching it, but I couldn't find its contours. It was stiff and slimy, like a frog-skinned bone. It could feel me, and I knew it. It was reacting with revulsion and hatred; the sun was a giant baleful eye burning my eyes inside the hood. It could see me, and I watched the thoughts in its face, choosing the moment to strike and stamp me out like the loathsome vermin I had become when I chose to invade its body.

Still stroking, still caressing, but with a trace of eagerness, of gathering passion, of consuming ardor. Getting ready, ready, ready for the climactic moment.

The scalpel handle coming down on my neck.

I couldn't breathe, my windpipe was trapped beneath my spine and closed, I was choking to death, my neck was bending, my spine was stretching, I had to break, but I couldn't scream because I didn't have the breath, I couldn't suck in air, couldn't get it out, I was on the verge of extinction, of breaking, of . . .

—Black out and *give it to me* . . .

I couldn't hear for the blood beating in my eardrums, I couldn't hear because there was no oxygen getting to my brain, I was fighting for air, for my senses, for my sanity.

—BLACK OUT ! ! !

I did.

I opened my eyes and could see absolutely nothing. I was hot and wet. And very tired. My body was strained as though it had been through terrible tortures. The wetness was sweat. It had poured out of me. But not on my face. There the wetness was cold water. There was a damp cloth on my face. As I blinked my eyelids, it was removed, and I looked up into Eve's face.

"You went out like a light," she said.

That I already knew.

"When?"

"As soon as we were down."

"We're down?"

"Yes."

But I knew that couldn't be. I'd blacked out after no more than a few minutes. We were more than a million miles away.

"What happened?" I asked. "I don't remember."

"Nothing happened. It was a rough ride, and I thought for a time we might all be dead. I could see Nick, and he was a corpse already, just waiting for deep-space to come in and claim him. But you just flew the ship. You shed your sweat and tears, but you flew the ship. We watched the strain in your movements, but they were always right. We landed."

"How long . . ." I began, and had to stop to clear my throat. "How long did it take?"

"Fifty-eight minutes. I counted them. We've been down about ten."

"Leave me alone," I said. She withdrew, taking the cloth with her.

I shut my eyes.

You did that?

—We did it. You found a little too much imagination. But you knew what to do, once your mind was submerged.

You knew what to do.

—I didn't need to. It was your brain that performed the operations. Your memories, your reflexes, your judgment. All I had to do was hold you together, make sure the machine worked.

I'm not a machine.

—You had to be a machine, to make that flight. Your mind was impairing your mechanical efficiency. That's why you had to black out.

If I'm so much of a handicap to my own body I wonder you haven't bothered to throw me out.

—I can't do that.

Well, I'm not sorry.

—You're not sorry I'm here, either.

You serve your purposes, I admitted. Could I have survived without him?

I opened my eyes again.

"Anything wrong?" Eve asked. She was still hovering around me.

"I ache."

DelArco shoved a cup of coffee into my hand. It occurred to me suddenly that someone had disconnected the hood and unclasped me. But I was too tired to worry. For the moment, we *seemed* safe, and I just didn't want to know about anything which opposed that impression.

"Charlot was right," said the captain. "We needed you."

"Yeah," I agreed modestly. "No other two guys could have done it."

I sipped the coffee for a moment or two, and it brought back my sense of bodily presence. Once that came back I began to worry about its continuation. I picked up the hood and looked at the world outside.

There wasn't a great deal to see. It was weird, but not frightening. I should have felt relieved—I could have dreamed up an awful lot of nastiness the world might have possessed.

I tuned in the famous *Lost Star* bleep. It came over loud and clear. I'd heard it before, of course, but only as a faint, illusory whisper. Now it was unmistakably real. Not a will o' the wisp. Not a siren song. It was a comfortable sound. Almost homely.

"Well," I said. "There's Captain Kidd's treasure. X marks the spot. Now get me something to eat, and let me rest for a while."

"Do you want a sleeper?" asked Eve.

"I don't need one. I'll take a pick-me-up in an hour or two, and then we'll go out into the wilderness. There's no point in hanging around too long. Tell Johnny to get the iron maiden ready.

"And," I added, "you better all remember that the slowest part of a spaceflight is the taxi into town. It might be all over bar the shouting, but don't hold your breath."

XX

There was, inevitably, a dispute about who was going to do what. Everybody wanted to go and nobody wanted to stay. I had my own reasons for not wanting to take anybody along, but delArco sure as hell wasn't going to let me get first look at the *Lost Star*. He still thought this was his joyride.

Finally, the argument had to reach its most rational solution. Somebody had to stay with the ship, and that somebody had to have some kind of chance to take the ship back if the landing party didn't make it. Which pointed the finger at Rothgar and Eve. Rothgar was no hero, and he was well satisfied, but Eve pleaded that there was only one *competent* pilot aboard. Unfortunately, she was reminded, said competent pilot was also the resident expert on alien territory, and hence had to go. We took Johnny along as well, against my better judgment. But delArco was the captain, and the arguments against weren't wholly convincing.

And so it was that three of us set forth in the iron maiden—a sort of amphibious tank designed and built on Penaflor, and supposedly the last word in transport for alien worlds. Penaflor has an unnaturally high regard for the efficacy of armor plating, which testifies to a military bent in its attitude. I'd never been in such a monstrosity before, so I was suspicious of its utility. But it was a lot faster than walking, and the only other alternative was to take the *Swan* up again and stooge around in atmosphere searching for the wreck. I certainly didn't want to do that

—mutilated space was bad enough without having to cope with atmosphere as well. And it was all too obvious that the effects of the distortion were as great on the surface as they were in space.

True enough, the surface didn't actually jump up and down—much. The wind wasn't violent enough to be called worse than capricious. But there was life here—life in extreme abundance, just as one might expect in an earth-type atmosphere. *Everything* that lived here was both a rhythmic and a facultative metamorph.

Which meant, in simple terms, that as the distortion waves came in from the contortive domain, the life forms co-opted the energy of the waves. Only immovable objects can resist forces of that magnitude. Iron maidens and spacesuits could stand firm against the distortion, just as they could keep out sunlight and hard radiation. But a life system can't evolve in an iron box. It can't just keep local conditions at barge-pole length. It has to live with them. Ergo the life forms lived off the distortional energy. They absorbed the inconstant flow, chaneled it, and employed it. Their only problem was a superabundance of supply. They had to invent ways of using it which weren't strictly necessary, in the empirical sense.

And so they perpetually changed shape.

Every distortion wave—their frequency varied from one every ten minutes to half a dozen a minute—occasioned a complete revision of the landscape. That was the rhythmic part. In addition, the life forms could use stored energy to make extra changes in between waves. Every bioform was as fluid as it wanted to be. It could be any shape it wanted, or none at all, just so long as it didn't try to hold one more than a moment or two.

And with a superabundant supply of warp energy from the solar domain, there was no limit to the profusion of life except life itself. The metamorphic system, I reasoned, must make for very fast evolution, but evolution in only one direction. The entire purpose of the metamorphosis was the *passive* aborption of energy. Conquest by submission and acceptance. But did this mean that we—as invaders—were safe from danger? Probably not—a pitfall is a very passive kind of trap.

We had not gone far before I noticed that the life forms

were not as versatile as I had at first supposed. There were only limited *types* of shape they could adopt. It must be something to do with the ordination of the stress-patterns. There were no sharp edges or straight lines, no axial joints. Cylinders and spheres were apparently preferred, but unduloids and catenoids were permissible, and several times I saw mobius-twisted entities which I took to be nodoids.

At first, I thought such a life system would lend itself very easily to the evolution of intelligence, but I later realized that this would be well-nigh impossible. Intellect necessarily involves some kind of mediation between stimulus and reaction: in the human instance it is rationalization. There are races which don't rationalize—which have no memories and no language—but which still might be classified as intelligent, but they *do* have a pseudo-emotional system acting as interpreter for physical signals, and some kind of decision-making apparatus which is modifiable by purely introspective means which have nothing to do with Pavlovian conditioning. They don't work by pure reflex. This life system did. There could be no gap between stimulus and reaction. There was no gap into which intelligence could fit.

All in all, I decided that this might well be the safest biosphere it had ever been my pleasure to tamper with. Whatever I did, it seemed, it could do only one thing: let me. However, I retained my caution and a respectable portion of my suspicion. Both delArco and I wore guns. Johnny—who had been delegated to remain with the vehicle—had a veritable arsenal beneath his fingertips. Firepower, of course, was something else much beloved of the nasty-minded people of Penaflor.

I didn't believe in wandering around inside a portable fort myself. It's one thing to carry a little tiny gun for the purpose of saving oneself from occasional embarrassment. It is quite another to have a kid, alone for the first time on a rather disturbing alien world, sitting on enough blast to evaporate a continent. That's a lot to ask of anybody's sense of judgment. And, of course, aliens are exactly the same as humans in one respect: whatever they do to make you shoot at them, they do a hell of a lot worse *after* you've shot at them. It takes a great deal of maddening or scarifying to make me shoot, but you couldn't depend on a kid like Johnny to show anything like that restraint. It's all right to order someone not to fire unless absolutely necessary, but you so rarely find out what absolute necessity is until afterward, which is ipso facto too late.

We made good time over the first hundred miles, and nobody bothered us. There was a distinct instrument flicker caused by the distortion field despite our shielding, but we couldn't get lost while we had the bleep. Radio communication with the ship was loud and clear, but a hundred miles isn't all that far, and we had several hundred still to go. We traveled, for the most part, over vegetation which was as keen to change color as shape, so that one minute we'd be driving along a bright blue valley with yellow spots, and the next it would be checkered red and black. I never saw the ground, the cover was so thick, but our wheels could feel it plainly enough—the vegetation beneath our wheels collapsed flat at our touch, and did its level best to get out from under. The plant carpet was dense but not tall—it barely came up to our mudguards.

I kept a constant watch on the terrain. It was so boring that it took a considerable amount of concentration to keep my attention there, but I didn't begrudge the effort of will. I failed to spot a single "higher" life form. No herd-consumers, no fliers, no fast movers. So there was no standard I could apply to the system to make it more comprehensible. On sane, sensible worlds, one can apply simple rule of thumb. Spot a slinky quadruped with big fangs and you know a little worry could be productive. Spot an absurd little creature stood on his back end waving a fist at you, and you know that worry is mandatory. The biggest danger *here* was that if there were anything which would bear worrying about, I wouldn't recognize it.

Things began to get difficult when we reached what looked like a gigantic flat plain. We had a fairly bumpy ride down to it, and from up above it looked like an endless mottled carpet, with colors flowing and fusing like an oil-slide. Close to us, we could see the leaves and the tendrils and the flowers changing too, dwindling away or bursting forth, shriveling and exploding, caught in helpless, purposeless gaiety by their relentless dancing master. But further away we could see nothing of shape—only color and preternatural flatness. The plain stretched clear to the horizon on three sides of us. Far away to our right, the sun was beginning to sink. Its inconstant light flared and faded, its diameter changed and blurred. Prominences were clearly visible in dazzling white and harsh, electric yellow.

Johnny eased us down the slope—where I saw bare rock protruding from the living sheath for the first time—and onto the plain. Where we promptly stopped.

"The wheel won't grip," he said. "I'm going down. Sinking."

"You're not sinking, you're floating," I told him. "This is the sea."

"Covered with plants?"

"Why not? Even on nice, normal worlds there are Sargasso Seas. Surface weed, extending skin, clustering plant islands. Thousands of square miles, on a lot of worlds. This isn't unusual."

He switched on the turbines, and the screws began to shove us laboriously through the tangle. It was the water rather than the plants which slowed us down. The matted vegetation put up not the slightest resistance to our passage. It changed to accommodate us—only too willing to oblige. Very polite.

"How far to the other side?" asked delArco morosely. He was bored stiff.

"Who knows? Maybe the *Lost Star* is moldering full fathom five on the seabed. Better call the *Swan* and tell them we won't be home for tomorrow's supper, let alone today's."

The captain laconically informed Eve that we'd hit treacle and might be considerably slowed.

"In the meantime," I suggested, "let's all remember that patience is a virtue, and very character-building."

The sudden drop in our pace made five hundred miles seem like a very long way. I'd been glad, last night, that I'd managed—or the wind had managed—to set down so close. On a planetary scale, five hundred miles is the edge of the bull's eye.

"We could play cards," said Johnny. "Or guessing games."

"If *you're* getting bored," I said, "let someone else drive."

"Who's driving?" he replied. "I just sit here. We're setting a dead straight course over dead level water in dead weather. Who needs to drive?"

"Never mind," I consoled him. "We might meet a sea monster."

Nobody was amused. I'm strictly a laugh-in-the-face-of-death humorist. When things are depressingly normal, sardonic irony becomes just as ordinary, and just as depressing.

I worried about the real possibility of meeting a sea monster for a little while, but pretty soon worry as a whole had lost both its flavor and its bite. Nothing was happening. Nothing even looked like happening. It didn't even look like rain.

I had to content myself with thinking how nice it was to let somebody else do the driving, and how this was the best chance I'd had to relax since I'd been picked up by the *Ella Marita*.

We had to take shifts at the wheel while we plugged steadily on across the ocean—for ocean it was, not just a salt lake or a channel between land masses. The limitlessness of it began to get heavy on the nerves. Eventually, I reasoned, we had to come to the end. The *Lost Star* couldn't *really* be under water, if her bleep was still going. If she was down at all, she couldn't be in perfect condition. And spaceships are designed to keep air in, not to keep water out. If she'd survived for eighty years, then she was high and dry.

The sun was still descending with reluctant lethargy to the horizon. Local daylight could last about fifty hours, all told, I estimated—which meant we had another eighteen or so. Local night might be longer or shorter, but I judged that it would most likely be the same length. The coordinates descriptive of the world's identity (which Alachakh had given us along with those defining its position) registered no axial tilt at all. I was prepared to doubt Caradoc's measurements (they were a long way away when they made them) but the fact that we'd contrived to set down so close suggested that they weren't far out.

I imagined that even during the night, there might be

light enough to see by. The afterglow of the sun would leave a long twilight because of the light-bending which took place in the distortion field. But even so, night wouldn't be as *comfortable* as day. Alien night is always a bad place to be.

In the meantime, the *Lost Star* bleep crept closer all the time. The sun set while we were still not clear of the sea. I asked whether anybody wanted to wait out the night where we knew we'd be safe, but the suggestion met with a derisory reception. I didn't think much of it myself. The sooner we got to the wreck, back, and away out of the Drift, the better we'd all feel. Two days sitting in the iron maiden was a lousy idea.

I was right about the night's darkness not being too intense. Although moonless, the world was ideally orientated to receive what illumination was available. We were pointed at a fairly light-dense sector of the Halcyon core, and a tight-knit cohort of thirty close suns cast an unsteady but welcome light. Like a great curtain, the gaping cavern of the core hung across the sky, shedding light that was pale, but sufficient. The horizon glowed white, surrounding us like a vast silvery ring set with a jewel-like flare at the point where the sun had vanished.

The colors in the weed around us—I thought of it as seaweed although there was no significant difference between the land and the sea plants—dulled to indigos, maroons, bronzes, and grays. Nothing pale, nothing bright, but we could still perceive the macabre dance of shape and hue.

Our distance from the *Lost Star* crept down through fifty miles, and forty.

I began to think again about what her cargo would be, and what I was going to do when I found it. By now, of course, I knew what the cargo was. Alachakh must have reasoned it out as well, but he hadn't told me in so many words because he couldn't be sure. It was easy enough to put myself in the place of a starship captain who—eighty years ago—had happened on the remains of an unknown civilization out beyond the rim. I knew what the *other* starship had brought back from similar missions. I knew what the most valuable thing in the galaxy was, so far as that captain's imagination had been concerned. And I knew that, ironically, that cargo would be completely worthless today, save to give away one single well-kept secret. Worthless, that is, in terms of contribution. In terms of price, I had no doubt that certain people would still be willing to pay a fortune for it, unseen.

Twenty miles from the *Lost Star* we came up out of the sea. Johnny and I were both dozing at the time, so we hadn't noticed the cliffs come looming up, and delArco hadn't thought it worthwhile disturbing us in order to tell us. He accelerated up the beach as soon as the wheels found purchase, and the jerk woke us both up.

He had to turn in order to search for an incline we could ascend. The cliff face looked sheer and savage—and unbroken.

This shore presented quite a different aspect. To judge by what we'd already seen, this land was bleak and inhospitable. Plants grew, but they grew high rather than wide. There was no anchorage to be found in the hard igneous rock, save in furtive crevices, and where the plants could grow, they chose to reach upward rather than laying prostrate over the implacable surfaces which offered them nothing. The plants either could not or would not drown this land as they had the first—here there was room to move. Here there was intermittent constancy.

The way delArco chose—had to choose, for there was no other—was sheer and bumpy. But the iron maiden was built to take it. Once or twice, I worried lest we slip backward, but she was a tenacious beast, and climbed the cliff with dogged insistence. Once on top of the cliff, we saw that our return to land wasn't going to enable us to make much better time. The landscape was broken and blasted. The vegetation was tall and clumped at all levels. There was nothing flat here—just a series of jagged surfaces meeting one another at all angles. The sum of the angles was a gentle upslope leading away from the cliff ledge. But there was no roadway, no easy path. It would be climb and crawl, almost as much down as up, ridge and gully and hump and crack, all the way up to the top of a mountain.

"It's an island," said delArco. "Part of a chain of volcanic origin." He pointed away to the right and left where, from our vantage point on the ledge, we could see other somber cones limned black by the dim painted sky.

"Where's the ship?" I asked, leaning forward from the back seat to see the instrument panel.

DelArco pointed up the mountain. "If I judge the distance right," he said, "it's on the plateau. Or in the crater, as the case might be." I ran my eyes along the jagged ridge which was, to our eyes, the topmost limit of the mountain. There was no way of telling what lay beyond the wall of rock. It could hardly be a live volcano if the *Lost Star* had been peacefully bleeping away therein for eighty years. But how deep a hole there might be we couldn't tell.

"Can we get up it?" I asked.

All three of us studied the slopes carefully.

"I don't know," said delArco. "But I should think so."

"You can't go mountain climbing in a tank," said Johnny. "It's not so much the getting up as the coming back down again." Which, of course, was a shrewd observation.

"It's not the most sensible expedition to undertake in a spacesuit, either," I told them. "Rock is sharp."

We eased forward, picking our way along gullies and over boulder-strewn rises, looking for a better view rather than making progress.

It was obvious that we would have to make some attempt at getting a good deal closer to the summit. It ought to be possible—it was a very big mountain, but it wasn't outstandingly high.

Looking around, I could see one or two of the living conglomerates moving within themselves. That was natural, of course, with their constant change of shape and reorientation of internal components, but in the gloom I got the impression that they were somehow stirred to action by our nearness—discussing us, watching us.

The captain moved the maiden forward as best he could, punctuating his efforts with occasional swearing—an uncharacteristic symptom of annoyance. I left the problem of getting down again to hope and providence. If the iron maiden failed us, she failed us and that was that. We'd have to swim home. Until then, we had to trust her to carry us where we needed to go.

Johnny took a short shift for a few hours which brought us to within three miles, and I took her a further two.

Things got more difficult all the time, and at the end of my shift I decided that we might as well leave it at that.

We all suited up—Johnny too, in case of emergency. We called the ship. Radio communication was very poor, but we could make ourselves understood.

"Right," I told Johnny. "You can hear us talking through the call unit. Leave the channel completely open. *Don't do anything.* You should be perfectly all right sitting here. If anything happens to us, we'll tell you what to do. If we don't tell you, don't do it. Sit tight and wait. If we don't come back, go home. Don't come after us because whatever happened to us would be bound to happen to you. You can't be forearmed unless you're forewarned."

"There's no point in me leaving you," he said. "We'd never *get* home."

"You stand a damn sight better chance than if you come after us. Eve can pilot the ship, even in deep drift. All she has to remember is to fly *slowly.* Anything I can do at two thou, she can do at two hundred. It might take you months, but home you *can* go. I'm not indispensable."

"Cut it out," said delArco. "What the hell's the point? We'll be back in a matter of hours. What can happen?"

"I don't know," I told him. "If I did, it *wouldn't* be necessary."

"Great," he said. "Let's get moving, if you're quite ready."

We opened the inner door and crammed ourselves into the lock—both at once so we needn't sterilize the interior in between transfers.

Outside, I felt almost naked for a moment or two. There's no doubt that armor plating has psychological power, even if its value is overrated.

But soon another feeling replaced the brief breath of insecurity, and that was a strange kind of familiarity. Almost nostalgia. Here was Grainger, standing in a suit in the alien night, ready to walk away into the unknown in search of money.

"Lead on," invited delArco. That was the real pioneer spirit emerging in the captain's character. You go first and I'll kill whatever kills you.

The first thing I did was to go to the nearest patch of metamorphic bioforms and peer into it at close range. The leaves, which writhed and flexed like fluttering fingers as they changed their form, were teeming with animal life, which likewise changed in phase with the plants. Most of the tiny animals were bulbous or vermiform, seemingly soft-bodied and legless—suckers or mucous gliders. Such was the profusion and confusion that I almost went cross-eyed trying to pick out exotic forms as they appeared and disappeared.

"Watch your feet," I said to delArco. "The plants have millions of tiny friends. All feeding off the living flesh, I imagine, and adapted to a dozen or more different morphs. Maybe each bug has a cycle tied to a specific plant morph cycle, but maybe not. I'd assume that wherever your eye rests there's something which could and would eat you if it got the chance. Don't let your suit get ruptured just on account of the breatheable air."

"That's what I like about you," said delArco. "You always look for the worst possible contingency."

"That's right," I said. "No other way makes sense."

As I've already said, rock climbing in spacesuits is nobody's idea of fun. Micropunctures are *especially* dangerous where the air is good. A tiny rip might not even give you the warning you need in order to do something about it. So I was inclined to tread very carefully indeed. DelArco naturally grew impatient. He *knew*—because it said so in the manual—that spacesuits are unrippable. The specifications clearly say that the material will stand up to anything. But you'll notice that the insurance doesn't cover you for mountain climbing, acid damage, and hostile aliens. The only reason the premiums are so cheap is because a lot of people never come back to claim.

The captain forged ahead. I briefly contemplated the idea that it might be immensely convenient if his spacesuit *did* rip, and I could go on to the *Lost Star* alone. But you can't go around shooting people in the back. It's antisocial.

Because he was ten or twenty yards ahead the whole way up to the lip, he was the first to peer over into previously unknown territory. He stood dramatically on the skyline, hoping to be the first human to clap eyes on the eighty-year-old wreck of the *Lost Star,* that fabulous legend of the spaceways.

Unfortunately, we couldn't see a damn thing except

jungle. *Real* jungle, this time. In fact, denser jungle than I'd ever seen before, on the couple of hundred worlds I'd touched.

It was a plateau rather than a crater, although it was about concave enough to be described as a vast shallow saucer. It was perhaps five miles in diameter, which put the *Lost Star* a lot nearer our edge than the far one.

"You there, Johnny?" I asked.

"I'm listening."

"We're standing on the lip now."

"I can see you."

"Can you get a precise enough fix on the *Lost Star* to tell me exactly how far she is?"

"Not exactly, no. About a thousand yards, I'd say. Give or take sixty." Sixty yards might be a long way in there, I mused.

"Give me the direction on your instruments, and my direction along your line of sight." He did so, and I checked the direction on my own compass. I also set my pedometer to zero. One of the reasons that spacesuits are nowhere near as efficient as their makers claim is that they're cluttered up inside with useless junk like pedometers.

"Did you manage to get through to Eve?" I asked.

"Yes."

"Everything all right?"

"Yes."

"OK then, here we go. Ready, Captain?"

DelArco nodded. I expelled my breath slowly, and looked around. I wished it were daylight. There was light enough, and I'm not habitually scared of the dark—even alien night—but I always prefer to walk into the jaws of death while the sun's shining. It makes the whole toothy appearance of the world seem more cheerful.

We plunged down into the mass of living confusion. It was quite unlike being in a forest or a jungle on any other world. Naturally, there's just barrier, and you have to hack and batter your way through it—fighting like crazy for every inch. But this stuff yielded to a bitter look. It didn't need much persuading. The trouble was that there was too much *of* it to yield that easily. It couldn't get out of our

way, because there was nowhere to go. And yet our every
touch was an abomination. Our presence and our progress
would cause the plants which we touched unbearable pain.

So what, I wondered, would they do?

What *could* they do?

After five minutes in that place, with the damn things
writhing away from under my feet and around my body,
panic-stricken but helplessly caged, I was feeling *sorry* for
the bloody things.

For some time, we weren't quite out of our depth in the
stuff, but it was clear that we'd soon be completely en-
tombed by the dream-like formlessness. We each had a
light mounted in our helmets, but they weren't made for
general illumination. They had a tight, bright beam for
working on the outsides of ships in deep-space. My lamp
cast a circle of light big enough to fit both hands into, but
it wasn't very useful. Happily, the instruments inside my
helmet—most notably the compass—had luminescent dials.

We plugged on. Captain delArco was just behind me
and—without quite clutching my hand—was sticking to
me for dear life. He said absolutely nothing, but I didn't
need to be told that he was scared rigid by the blackness
and the feel of the furtive, glutinous chaos through which
we moved. Myriads of tiny creatures were accidentally
transferred from the plants to me, and I hoped none of
them was adapted for chewing tough plastic. But most of
them had no intention whatsoever of staying with me for
longer than cruel fate dictated. They couldn't get away
fast enough. Some stuck fast, and I assumed that these
wouldn't be getting away at all. This trip was wreaking
its own special brand of havoc. Every hundred yards or so
I had to wipe my faceplate.

With three hundred yards still to go, I stopped to consider the details of my master plan. The captain was glad
of the rest, but remained terrified.

"Johnny?" I said.

"Yes."

"Everything is fine. Looks like no trouble. I'll call again
when I reach the ship."

"Check."

I moved slightly, and delArco placed his hand on my

shoulder, I wasn't sure whether he wanted more rest, or whether he just didn't want to risk losing sight of me. He didn't say a word. I brushed away his hand, but stood still. He sagged a little, and tried to lean on the plants. But of course they wouldn't entertain the notion, and just gave way. He fought for the balance he'd so carelessly committed to the nonexistent support, lost the fight, and fell over. I left, in a hurry. There was a moment's dreadful pause, when I thought he might not panic, and then he screamed.

"*Grainger!*"

"What's the matter?" I inquired, not pausing in my stride.

"I've lost you." Fear dripped from every syllable.

"Well, don't panic," I reprimanded him primly. "That's the thing to avoid. You're not helpless. You know where the ship is. The one thing we mustn't do is stagger around in this stuff. We might get lost."

"Come back here!"

"I haven't gone anywhere." I lied. "I can't be more than a few feet away. But don't start fumbling around for me. Use your compass and your pedometer. You can get to the ship."

"I was following *you*," he wailed. "I don't know the way, and I don't even know what a pedometer *is!*"

"Don't get hysterical," I told him. "You heard the compass bearings Johnny gave me. I assure you I didn't lose the straight line. You don't need the pedometer. Just keep going in a straight line, and you'll reach the ship."

"Why can't you come back for me?"

"Because I'd lose the straight line and the direction. I assure you that my way is best. I'm going on now. If you start now as well, we'll probably only be a matter of three feet apart the whole way."

"Grainger, *please!*" He was petrified. Which was good. I was relying on the fact that even given the right compass bearing, he *still* wouldn't be able to find the ship. Not before I'd had time for a good look and a chance to act, anyway.

"I'm moving, Captain," I said sweetly. I hoped that my voice didn't betray any of the satisfaction I felt. But call circuits distort in a most convenient manner.

Behind me, delArco began to sob.

Poor bastard, I thought. You poor bastard.

Then my light fell upon a human face, and it was my turn to be terrified.

XXI

I wiped my faceplate clear of little beasties with a quick stroke of the back of my hand. As I did so, the circle of light shifted. So did the face. It stayed where I could see it. It stared vacuously at my silver-clad form.

"Doctor Livingstone, I presume?" I said.

I put out my hand, and he disappeared. Just *gone,* into nothingness, or into . . . plantness.

"I have a horrible suspicion," I confided to the world in general, "that things are not as they should be. We have been trampling on somebody's toes, and . . ."

I was rudely interrupted by Captain delArco, who screamed again.

"Shut up, Captain," I said tiredly. "It's not real. Just the plants. They can change shape, remember."

He didn't stop crying. His nerves were pretty bad.

I waited.

"What the hell's happening?" Johnny wanted to know.

"The jungle's making faces at us. It can't hit us, or hurt us, or call us names. So it's making faces at us. I think the captain is frightened."

The calmness of my voice and the scorn inherent in the last remark brought delArco back to his senses. "I'm all right," he said heroically. "I was startled, that's all."

"Great," I said. "I'm on my way again."

But the moment I moved again, I was a stimulus. The jungle had got an idea, and it had worked—stopped me dead in my tracks. It wasn't about to give up.

There was another face, and another, and another. But

shock tactics had lost their effect. I was no longer impressed. I walked straight through them. This time, the jungle wasn't so slow with its inventiveness. The faces changed expression. From vacuousness, they passed through fear and pain and agony. I watched the face—always the same face—grow thinner, watched the flesh whiten and tauten about the bones, watched it begin to peel from the face, watched it dissolve and flow and writhe. I watched the death and decay of a human being. Wherever my lamp fell, there it was. As long as I moved, the continuity was maintained. No rest for the wicked.

—It's one of the crew of the *Lost Star*, supplied the wind. It's something they've actually seen and experienced. It took them time to recognize you as human. That's why there was a delay.

So why are they showing me? I asked. Are they threatening me with the same fate? Trying to scare me to death? It won't work.

—Forget about trying to prove how tough you are, the whisper replied. They aren't trying to hurt you. They're like everything else on this world—just plain and simple reaction. To every stimulous, they have a reaction. It's the whole of their existence. They can't fail to react. They can't fail to react specifically. This is all they need to do —from their point of view—to cancel you out. You were hurting them before, as an invader with no programmed response. But not now. They've made up their minds. They've blotted you out of their existence plane. From now on, you're just an accident of providence. They don't care about *you*, Grainger. They won't hurt you. They can't even try.

Thank you, I said, you've taken a load off my mind.

Then I found the *Lost Star*.

She was still intact. The jungle was close up to her sides, but it didn't touch her. I paused for breath, leaning on the hull. She was a long, wide-bellied ship with big tailfins and solid wings. She wasn't ugly but she was outsize—Junoesque.

I knew as soon as I realized just how big she was that my plan to lose delArco wouldn't pay off. She was no needle in a haystack. No matter how nervous or incompetent delArco might be, he couldn't possibly stagger around

forever without finding her. I cursed the fashion that had
made them build so big eighty years ago. Today's ships
were much more compact and just as functional. As the
unknown universe had shrunk—in importance rather than
in size—so had human gestures of defiance.

I wandered along her length, looking for the lock. I
didn't find it on my side of the ship. When I reached the
fins, I used them to climb on top of her. The plants grew
only two or three feet taller than she lay, but it was enough
to hide her from the crater's top. From on top of her I
couldn't see very much except jungle. Not that there was
anything to see.

I walked along the length of the ship again, peering
over onto the side I hadn't seen. Again, no lock. There was
only one place it could be, and that was underneath. I
swore silently. The time I'd gained from delArco was
slowly draining away—wasted if I couldn't gain access to
the ship's cargo hold. I jumped down at the nose, forgetting quite how high I was because I couldn't see the
ground. The plants, of course, did little or nothing to
break the impact, and I turned my ankle. I had to hobble
painfully along the side of the ship, wasting yet more time.
Then I got down on my hands and knees and began a
fast crawl beside the underbelly of the ship. I prayed that
when I found it, the door would be either open or missing, so that I could get in with a minimum of effort. I was
three-quarters of the way along when I found it at long
last, hidden by the curve of the hull from the top, but not
as inaccessible as I'd thought. Although shut, it was
hinged on the undermost side. If I could get it open, I
could certainly crawl in.

"Grainger," said delArco's voice. "Have you reached
her yet?"

"No," I replied. "How are you doing?"

"OK." He'd regained his composure. I swore silently.

I lay on my back and scrambled underneath to get into
the right position to manipulate the handle of the door.
The door came open and fell heavily on my chest. I swore
again—audibly—and squirmed out. With great care, I inserted myself into the narrow gap between door and hull.
I wormed my way in, hoping that I didn't damage my
suit. Then, bracing myself against the walls of the airlock,

I shut the outer door. I opened the inner one and climbed thankfully into the corridor. The ship had "up" along her vertical axis, like the *Hymnia*, but ship's gravity was off and the shaft was now a tunnel. I searched with my lamp for the light switch, found it beside the lock, and pressed it. The lights came on.

I paused on the rim of the hatchway, then carefully drew my gun, adjusted the beam, pointed it at the unlocking mechanism of the outer door, and fused the catch. That, I thought, should take Captain delArco some little time to sort out. In the meantime, let us see what is to be seen.

The corridor, meant for climbing up or down, wasn't wide enough to permit me to stand up. I had to crawl all the way to the control room.

"Grainger," said delArco.

"What now?"

"You must be there by now."

"I've found her," I admitted.

"Fine," he said. "Don't do anything. I'll be with you in a matter of minutes."

"Yes, Captain," I replied dutifully.

The control room was quite empty of human forms— dead or alive. I went rapidly to the controls. The computer was still alive, as was the bleep. I tried a couple of elementary call signs, to make sure I knew what I was dealing with. Then I flipped all the switches under the console, reducing the artificial brain to so much scrap metal, wiping out the whole of the data store—including the ship's log.

Well, I said to myself, it's only logical that before abandoning ship they should have reduced their power drain to a minimum, thus making the bleep last as long as possible. Nobody can tell whether the computer was killed now or eighty years ago. Can't pin *that* on me.

I began to check the cabins, one by one. They were all quite empty.

The cargo hold was sealed tight, and I hadn't a clue where to look for the keys. In all probability, one of the crew had pocketed them before they tidied up and jumped ship. I hadn't time to go searching for keys, though. Once delArco found the ship it wouldn't take him long to cut through the outer door.

About as long as it took me to cut my way into the cargo hold, in fact.

I pushed the door with the toe of my boot, and I felt the lock go under the pressure. I leaned my full weight on the door, making sure my suit didn't touch the hot patch, and it gave way slowly.

The hold was unlighted, and I searched for a switch, but couldn't find one. I switched on the helmet lamp again, and let the beam play over the cargo.

"I've found her," caroled delArco.

"Good," I said, with a marked lack of enthusiasm. "Where's the door?"

"Around the far side, underneath," I told him. There was no point in keeping quiet now. I hadn't gained the time I needed. Maybe I could still destroy the cargo, but I certainly couldn't hide the fact that I'd done so. It was now a choice between serving Titus Charlot faithfully to the end, or risking all kinds of unpleasant consequences. While I was hesitating, I let my eyes roam casually over the legendary *Lost Star* cargo.

The hold was crammed tight with books and papers and files full of film and notes. The books were old—maybe millions of years—but they still held together. There were some small items of artwork—mostly carvings and colored metal-prints. There was some synthetic fabric as well. But by far and away the bulk of the cargo was knowledge—alien knowledge. The most salable commodity of the eighty-year-old galaxy. High-priced today as well, of course, although with what New Alexandria already had under its belt, the desperation had drained out of the market, and familiarity had knocked prices way down. In these days, alien knowledge was merely a convenience. In those days, it had been a fashion. New Alexandria had an insatiable thirst for it, and every world in the human universe needed New Alexandria to have it, to translate it, to understand it. The galaxy had been really hooked on the stuff. Maybe it reduced the fear of the unknown to know that alien races were being dissected in our computers within days of discovery, to know that we were keeping abreast of the universe, no matter how big it was. Crazes like that die easy, but the long-term effects were just beginning. The integration of alien and human, the use of what New Alexandria had bought.

It was obvious all along what the *Lost Star* had carried —once I knew that she had found a dead world out there. There would be no King Solomon's Mines on a dead world—just small remnants of a civilization, the shards of its accomplishments. After all that time, there would be not a trace of everyday life left behind. The only things to have survived the tremendous lapse in time would be things which were indestructible—either accidentally indestructible because of careless use of materials, or purposely so, in terms of permanent records and what the people had deliberately *built* to be indestructible. And what the *Lost Star* had picked up was anything she could scavenge that might tell something about Myastrid and her people.

And it was all useless. For what could Myastrid tell us that Khor could not? No technological secrets, no philosophies, no sciences. All this had been passed on from the parent world to the colony on Khor. And from the Khormonsa to New Alexandria. It was no accident that the first integration of intellectual achievements had been between Khormon and Human. The Khor-monsa had been very forthcoming about all aspects of their life and civilization. Apparently, they had wanted to keep only one secret. There was only one thing that they did not want the prying humans to discover.

I do not pretend to understand Khormon thinking. I call their insistence pride, and their manner politeness, but these are human words which refer to human attributes. They can have no precise relevance to alien peoples. I do not know why the keeping of this one secret was of such import. But that they had gone to some effort to keep it was obvious, if the majority of their own people did not know it. Perhaps, if they managed to destroy Myastrid, and suppress the *Lost Star* cargo, even those who knew about it would be able to forget it. And the Khor-monsa could be, in practical truth, the men of Khor.

By the Law of New Rome, this cargo belonged to Titus Charlot. His consortium owned the *Hooded Swan*. They had commissioned her. In other systems of law, the cargo might have belonged to the Khor-monsa. Myastrid was not a derelict ship, but a world. Its people lived on, as the Khor-monsa. The *Lost Star* had not salvaged these books, but stolen them. But the contemplation of such legal and ethical niceties was not helpful. I already knew what I wanted to do. I wanted to burn every last page.

Not because Alachakh had wanted me to, although that was a good reason. Not because I respected the Khor-monsa, although that was a fact. Because I wanted to spite Titus Charlot. Because I *wanted* to cheat him, and rob him of what little glory I could. And because I wanted to destroy the legend of the *Lost Star*. I wanted the silly story to come to absolutely nothing, to make a fool of the whole bloody human race. Except me. And also because it was a good joke.

Of such things are motives made. Nobility and altruism are unknown in the human race.

So when Captain delArco stuck his head out of the inner hatchway, I jammed my gun up against his faceplate.

XXII

He stared at it so hard his eyes crossed.

"Be quiet, Captain," I hissed, in conspiratorial tones. And then, to Johnny: "Johnny! This is Grainger. Do exactly as I say and don't ask questions. Don't say a word. *Switch off the call circuit at the maiden.* Sit tight and don't move."

I didn't hear him cut out, of course, but I had to assume that he'd do as he was told.

"Now, Captain," I said. "Take it easy. Now, are you wired to that monitor on the ship?"

"You know I am."

"You're transmitting right now?"

"All the time."

"Then switch it off."

"I can't."

"Yes, you can. Laws of New Rome. Invasion of privacy. You have to be able to take yourself out of the monitor. So do it."

There was a pause.

"OK," he said, "it's off. But I've already seen you holding a gun on me. I've heard you tell me to switch off. You're in deep trouble."

Again, I couldn't actually know whether he'd switched off or not. I just had to assume he was cooperating.

"Now you can come out," I said.

As he did so, I relieved him of his gun.

"Are you going to explain?" he asked.

"But of course. I need your help and understanding.

161

I can't tell you everything, I'm afraid, but I'll tell you all
I can. The full story, abridged edition. OK? Well then . . ."

"This trip is a stupid stunt. Its sole purpose is to make
a fool out of the Caradoc Company and make capital out
of the joke. Everybody will laugh because nobody loves
Caradoc. In order to pull off this farcical trick, a pilot
named Grainger is obliged to risk his own life and several
others."

"Nobody forced you."

"Don't interrupt. And as for force, twenty thousand
with a penalty clause in case I die young is a powerful
lever. I'd call twenty thousand an awful lot of obligation.

"To continue with the sordid story, Grainger—while
willing to comply with the blackmail for reasons of self-
preservation—understandably fails to discover any strong
loyalty to his employers. He is very fond of his new ship,
but this only serves to make him that much less fond of
the people who wish to prostitute her into a performing
freak.

"He discovers that the owner is somewhat unbalanced,
and cares nothing about the ship or its crew, but only
about the credit due to him for his part in a complicated
scheme. His interests lie entirely in showmanship and vain-
glory. However, he relies upon others to go out and perform for him, and gather his glory. Grainger suspects that
Titus Charlot may have set him up to be clobbered with
the twenty thousand which he later volunteers to pay off.
Charlot certainly finds out very early that Grainger is back
in circulation, which implies that he has some contacts in
the Caradoc organization, or on New Rome. Grainger also
believes Charlot to be responsible for the attempt on his
life by a crocolid. He does not, of course, suggest that
Charlot paid the crocolid, but simply that he talked so
loudly about his ship and what it would do that Caradoc
was inspired with the idea of bumping off its pilot.

"In brief, Grainger does not like Charlot.

"Meanwhile, back at the plot, Charlot chooses as captain of ship a man calculated to get on Grainger's nerves.
Sole purpose of said captain is to keep all legal responsibility out of Grainger's reach. Ship's captain has all
sorts of authority under the Law of New Rome. Ship's
pilot has not. Captain is therefore a device to make sure

that Grainger can only do as he is told. Captain delArco is a puppet. He has been played for a sucker by Titus Charlot. In order to promote and maintain tension between the two men—so that the captain doesn't listen any more than is necessary to Grainger—Charlot also puts aboard one female, always guaranteed to provide tension, one engineer notorious for creating bad morale aboard his ships, and one crewman who wants to like everybody and only serves to highlight the differences between them.

"An unhappy Grainger then finds out that his closest friend—Alachakh—desperately wants to reach the *Lost Star*. His reason is so powerful that he is willing to kill himself in the attempt. That reason, of course, is an alien reason. You wouldn't understand it. Neither do I. I'm not asking you to believe that reason had any meaning as far as you or I am concerned. But it *was* a reason. It *is* a reason. And we have no reason. None at all. We're here at the whim of a megalomaniac.

"In part, you know, we killed Alachakh. It was us he was racing. He could have beaten Caradoc easily. But not us. We forced him to fly too fast. We made him fail in his mission. It was our fault that he died with his job unfulfilled. I'm not suggesting that because of that we have a duty to him. We don't owe him anything. But you can't forget him. You can't just imagine that he never existed. Because he did. And we were there when he died.

"I'm not going to tell you what Alachakh's reasons were. They were personal as well as alien. They'd mean nothing to you, and he didn't want me to tell anybody what they were. But I put to you this proposition: We can pull off Charlot's stunt. We can beat Caradoc, we can give him his chance to gloat. But we can also at one and the same time, fulfill Alachakh's purpose. We can do what he wanted to do.

"So what do we do?"

"That depends," answered delArco. "It sounds far too good not to have a catch. You're trying damned hard to sell me. What do we have to do in order to pull off this classic double?"

I licked my lips. "The *Lost Star*'s cargo is in her hold. I want to burn it. Every last vestige of it. And then I want you to corroborate my story that it never existed. That the whole thing was a myth. A lie."

"And what is the cargo?" There was a quality in his voice which suggested that he already suspected.

"Books. Alien books."

He nodded. "And you aren't going to tell me why you want them burned? Alien reasons?"

"Alien reasons," I agreed. "But I'll tell you a couple of things for free. One: these books contain no scientific or technological information which is not already available to New Alexandria. Two: the secret that I want kept is quite harmless. In human terms, it is practically meaningless. We can hurt no one by destroying this cargo, but we can help a lot of people on Khor."

"Do I get time to think?" he asked.

"Sure."

"Will you point those guns somewhere else."

I stuck them both into my belt. Then I sat back to wait. A few minutes passed, and he remained deep in apparent contemplation.

"There's no evidence that this cargo ever existed," I pointed out. "Nobody can pin anything on either of us."

"You're asking me to put a hell of a lot of trust in you."

"That's right," I agreed.

"What will you do if I refuse to help you?"

"Burn the books anyway."

"And me with them?"

"No. I'll take you home, and hope you change your mind on the way."

"And if I don't?"

"Then Titus Charlot will be very angry indeed. With both of us. But I'm not Titus Charlot. I don't leave a wake of corpses. It's your choice. If you won't help me, I'll do it on my own."

Then I crossed my fingers and sat back. I knew I would win. If anyone had tried to hand me a load of garbage like I'd just handed out to delArco, I'd have told them where to stick it. But Nick delArco was a *nice* man. People liked him. He was nice because he *wanted* people to like him. Even me. If he thought he could win me over by doing me a favor now, then he would. Of such things are motives made. We all have our human weaknesses.

"All right," he said finally. "Let's burn the books. You convinced me."

Logic is just our excuse for doing the things we want to do.

"Yes sir," I said.

"You can call me Nick," he said sardonically.

"That's right," I murmured. "We're friends, now."

XXIII

"You didn't want me in on this at all, did you?" he said. as we fed books to the fire in the burned-out drive chamber. "Leaving me in that forest and fusing the lock on the door."

"It might have been easier if you'd stayed lost."

"How did you propose to stop me finding the ashes once I *did* get here?"

"Close up the drive chamber and claim it was hot."

"What about the gauge?" he said, pointing at the radiation counter.

I grinned. "By the time I closed up, the chamber *would* have been hot."

"People get hurt messing about with atomics," he commented.

I continued to haul stuff out of the hold and pass it along to him. He threw it into the drive chamber. I'd decided to have the fire there anyway, for safety's sake. Just in case Caradoc ever did beat the odds and get here. The best place to hide trees is in forests, the best place to hide evidence of a fire is in the ashes of an older fire. When the *Lost Star* had come down, her engine had gone exactly like the *Hymnia*'s. It's the way dimension-hoppers nearly always go.

"You know," said delArco—he was very talkative now we were on the same side—"I'm not New Alexandrian, but I was brought up to their ways of thought. I was taught that burning books is the worst crime you can commit."

"Circumstances," I replied, "alter cases."

"Circumstances never seem to alter you."

"They do," I assured him.

"You always seem the same way to me."

"Yeah," I said. "And what way is that?"

"Untouched by human hand. Isolated. Alienated. And trying desperately to keep it up no matter how circumstances change."

"I just don't let things get to me, that's all. You can't if you live the way I do. If alien worlds once begin to reach you, you're as good as dead. Grounded, anyway, which is almost as good as dead. You have to stay steady. Lapthorn used to say I had no soul."

"I'm not talking about alien worlds reaching you," he said, as we tirelessly passed the books from hand to hand, "I'm talking about people. You don't let *them* touch you either."

"Where's the difference?" I countered. "Alien is alien is alien. People are alien to me."

"You're people too."

"So it's said."

"So you can't be alienated from yourself."

"Look," I said, pausing. "What's all this in aid of? Just because our purpose is one for the first time, there's no call for you immediately to start saving my soul from the pit of despair." I threw the next load twice as hard, for emphasis, but he caught it comfortably. He was a big man.

He shrugged. "You're inconsistent. You give me a long spiel about Titus Charlot's disregard for his crew, but you profess to a total disregard for everybody."

"I pointed out Titus Charlot's disregard for the *lives* of his crew," I said. "Not for their love and generosity. The less Charlot cares about my state of mind, the better I like it. It's my state of health I don't like him jeopardizing."

"You really think there's a lot of difference?"

"So OK," I said, unworried and unmoved. "I'm a real test for patience. Also understanding and faith in human nature. Maybe I'm no better than Titus Charlot. I didn't claim to be. What I said is still true, isn't it?"

He didn't bother to answer. We were almost through the cargo now—it hadn't taken nearly as long as I'd feared. The drive chamber was brimful of junk, and we were having to use a pretty powerful beam to make the stuff burn or melt, or otherwise render it unrecognizable. Myastridians built to last. The whole ship was full of smoke, and it must have been as hot as hell. Spacesuits come in very handy, now and again.

"What about the monitor tape back at the ship?" said delArco suddenly. "It has a rather embarrassing bit of conversation on it, just before it's switched off."

"You can chop the lot at the point where we entered the distortion field. Never can tell how these deep-space phenomena will affect delicate equipment, can you? Great shame the tape is blank from then on, isn't it? Charlot will simply have to rely on a word of mouth account of the finding of the *Lost Star*."

"I should think we'll find documents in the cabins. The crew isn't there—they jumped ship, sealed her up and went to live in the jungle, I suppose. They're not here, anyway—not even whitened bones. But they won't have taken their ship's papers with them. We'll get enough to establish where we've been. And as a centerpiece to the collection, we'll cut the nameplate out of the hull. A nice touch, don't you think? They can hang it up on a wall somewhere as an everlasting memorial to the conquest of the Halcyon Drift. They might even put a plaque underneath it with our names on. Wouldn't that be just wonderful?"

"We could take back the control levers as well," he suggested.

"You'd have cynical souls doubting their origin," I told him. "Anything that doesn't have *Lost Star* stamped on its backside won't convince the average skeptic. On the other hand, we could have a few thousand replicas made, and sell them off as holy relics."

"What are you going to tell Johnny?" he returned to the point. "He's going to be pretty curious about the way you cut him off."

"Pretend it never happened. Ignore it."

"You can't do that. He's bound to ask."

"Then we say that it seemed the best thing to do at the time. We considered it advisable, bearing in mind the circumstances. If he persists, tell him to shut up. Privileges of rank."

"So it's all worked out," he said.

"Certainly is," I replied. We threw the last of the books onto the fire, and I opened up with my gun again, using up the last of the charge ensuring that everything which could be destroyed would be. The walls of the drive chamber were slowly melting, the molten metal bubbling and streaming. The volume of the incandescent remains shrunk as ash shriveled away into the walls.

"Don't crack that piledriver," said delArco, in worried tones.

"Take more than a few thousand degrees to make any impression on *that* shielding," I assured him. "It's compact matter."

Finally, completely satisfied, I stuck the empty gun back into my belt. When the chamber cooled down, it would not look much different from the way it had looked when I'd first opened the door. A burned-out room doesn't suffer much extra for going through the same thing twice.

"We'll have to leave the main hatch open to let smoke out," I said, "but apart from that we can collect our souvenirs and leave her as we found her."

I went to the nose of the ship to carve out the nameplate, as I'd suggested, while delArco searched the cabins and the control room for official documents. When I'd finished with the nameplate, I went and cut off a couple of the control levers for good measure. I'd have liked to take more junk, but delArco's gun was almost empty by now, and I liked to hold a little power in reserve.

Last of all, I killed the *Lost Star* bleep. The siren of the spaceways was no more. Kaput, dead, finished. One legend, crushed beneath the heavy hand of reason. And that's almost the end of the story.

XXIV

Captain delArco woke me up. It was the first night I'd spent in a bunk in a coon's age, and I wasn't too pleased.

Luckily, he came straight to the point instead of sparing the time to be sarcastic.

"Four ships just entered the system," he said. "Caradoc ramrods."

"What do you want me to do?" I snarled. "Congratulate them on getting so close?"

"You said they'd never make it," he pointed out.

"I said it'd take months. It still will. They'll have to come through the contortive domain at walking pace."

"They aren't going to come through the contortive domain. They just bleeped us to tell us so. They weren't pleased when they found they'd been beaten to the punch."

"So?"

"The gist of the message was this: Captain Casorati of the Caradoc Company's ship *De Lancey* to the New Alexandrian *Hooded Swan*. We request you to transmit a statement renouncing all legal title to the cargo and effects of the *Lost Star*, surrendering same rights to the Caradoc Company in fair trade for instructions as to how to escape from the Drift. We feel it incumbent upon you to warn you that if you do not comply with this request, you will undoubtedly fall prey to the Drift."

There was an amazed silence for some three seconds. Then I burst out laughing.

"They're threatening to shoot us down!" I gasped.

"Ramrods threatening the *Hooded Swan*. That's the funniest thing I've heard in years."

"Those ramrods are armed," said delArco humorlessly.

"I don't care if they're packing planet-smashers," I said. "Do you have any idea how difficult it is to hit anything in space? Let alone *warped* space? There are millions of miles of bent emptiness between us and the Caradoc ships. How can they possibly throw a missile across that so accurately that we can't even dodge it?"

"Are you sure about that?"

"Of course I'm sure. In this space, they'd be lucky if they could hit a bloody star, let alone a spaceship. If they start shooting, they'll be far more likely to hurt themselves than to hurt us. I suggest you tell them that. But be polite. Assure them that we're very grateful for their kindness in offering to help us out, but we think we can make it on our own. We also thank them for their concern regarding our vulnerability but suggest they are far more likely to fall prey to the Drift than we."

I was still laughing when I got back to the controls, ready for lift.

I got an attack of pathological fear about five minutes before takeoff, but it was nothing to do with the Caradoc ships. I had to face the distortion field again. Last time, it had broken me. Could I beat it this time?

—We can take the ship out, the wind assured me.

You can bloody keep out of it. She's my ship and I'll take her out.

—You needed my help to get in.

I was too unconscious to refuse it.

—And suppose you black out again? You don't have to be ashamed of accepting help. I didn't do anything that you couldn't have done. You didn't *fail*. I used your body, your skill, your speed. You don't understand me at all. I'm not a threat to you. I'm not trying to take over from you. I am a new *part* of you. An extra faculty. A new talent.

I don't need you!

—*So what?* I *know* you don't need me. I never said you did. Of *course* you don't need me. But you've *got* me. How long is it going to take you to reconcile yourself to that fact? You—Grainger the lone wolf—are not alone anymore. You never will be again. Not ever, no matter how hard you try. We have to live with one another, you and I. It isn't a horrible curse. You aren't possessed by devils. I'm not going to feed on your brain, rob you of your body. I am *here*. *We* are here. *Can't you accept what that means?*

I don't like it, I said, and it's as simple as that.

And it was.

They quote Confucius as having said that if rape is inevitable, lie back and enjoy it. Well, lie back by all means, if you can't do anything else. But you can't and won't enjoy it, if rape is what it is. That's the beginning and the end of it.

—Grainger, said the whisper ominously, a lifetime is a long time.

Never mind, I told him, it'll soon pass.

Meanwhile, back in the real world . . .

The distortion field had drained slightly, knocking a hundred thousand miles or so off the shortest way out. But I wasn't sure if I should take that. Caradoc's missiles, if they really meant what they said, would surely take the shortest way in, and there was no point in taking needless chances, no matter how futile their threats might be. But which was I more afraid of: the proximity of Caradoc's missiles or a few extra seconds in the lesion?

After feeling the field from a sitting position—something I'd been unable to do on the way in—I decided that in all probability the shortest way out wouldn't be the easiest anyhow. I had to make maximum use of the field's energy to supplement our own. I plotted a rough arc about four million miles long—more than twice the minimum distance. This arc had the added advantage of pointing us away from the Caradoc ships instead of at them.

To dispel the clammy fingers of fear, I made Rothgar start the countdown early. As the count went down, the workings of my brain phased in on the ticking of the clock, and I lost my shakes.

We blasted our cannons, and lifted, and I raised her on the air, feeling for the pressure of the warp and whispering, "Once more into the breach, dear friends."

There was one second, two, three, and four while we climbed and accelerated out of atmosphere and into the crooked void, and then Caradoc let loose.

All four ships let go at once, and I stopped wondering whether they really meant business. It suddenly burst upon my tired brain exactly what they'd meant by "falling prey to the Drift." I'd made a mistake. I'd been wrong. All hell was on its way.

I judged the velocity of the missiles to be thirty thou or so. The possibility of a hit was negligible, and not worth considering. What *was* well worth considering was what they'd do to the contortive domain. They'd rip holes in space the size of stars. Core power would vomit out of the holes and the entire system would bleed energy and timespin and the foul fiend would walk the sky, gathering souls for his unearthly kingdom. . . .

With a savage adherence to their purpose, which company headquarters would no doubt find admirable, they fired everything they had as fast as they could, seeding the contortive domain. They didn't even bother to aim at poor little us.

"Load the flux," I yelled at Rothgar. "Load her every ounce she'll take and then some. If we transfer it'll be in no time flat, and we might never come down again. Damn the safety factors and give me *everything*."

Rothgar didn't even bother to reply. If I made transfer in this field we'd be ninety percent certain to blow up, and he knew it. Maybe more, carrying excess load in the flux. But I had to have the power. If I was caught short, we'd be one hundred percent dead.

In fours, the fours coming less than a second apart, the missiles plowed up the domain. I could feel the patterns of the field recoiling in horror at the shock. The whole warp bubbled up like a volcano getting set. I could feel the sun stretching her muscles as she woke up, preparing to yank open the floodgates and let all the power in the Drift flow into her cloak of screwed-up space.

One missile—*one*, out of forty or fifty—passed within a thousand miles or so of the *Swan*. It cut a path right past us and zoomed on, almost parallel to the way I'd wanted to go. I spared a split second to hope the thing wouldn't explode too soon, and I went after it.

The field was completely and hopelessly smashed. The storm was already flooding out of the heart of the star. The gates of hell were already yawning wide, and death was coming out to eat us up. The field was hanging in that strange half-instant when nothing was happening— when the old field had died and the new fury hadn't quite got here yet.

That half-instant was the only time I had.

As the missile hurtled through the shattering distortion field it literally ripped a hole in space—a long, hollow bullet wound in the fabric of the warp. I didn't know what was in that hole and I didn't care. It might be a time schism, or an undiscovered dimension. Going into it was like jumping down a well and hoping that it would be bottomless, and that I could emerge intact from another mouth. It was a tunnel to nowhere, but it was the only way out, and I wasn't hanging around.

I dragged the *Swan* from one path to the other by the scruff of her neck. If the distortion pattern had retained its integrity it would have ripped us apart. But it had already gone, and we were between the cage and the death wave. Pain convulsed my brain but not my hands, I hauled us into the tunnel, and I transferred.

The ship's gravity cut off, the lights went out, and the hood went blank. I was blind, but we flew. Practically instantaneous transition from low subcee to thirty thou. We were out of what had been danger before I had time to hope, and everything began to work again. The moment the image came back in the hood, I reacted. I couldn't change direction or slow us down because I didn't have the time. I raised a wing and contorted my body. I practically shaved the skin off the missile as I overtook it.

It exploded nearly a million miles behind us.

The thin distortion which ought to have been globing the outer system was completely gone. We were running inside that *empty* instant—the moment of transition.

At twenty-five thou I went away, and sustained the velocity for three minutes or more until—well clear of the system—I hit dirt and sanity, and had to slow down again.

We were well out of harm's way by then.

The *De Lancy* and her three ladies-in-waiting were not. They blew up.

Honi soit qui mal y pense.

"Well," I said. "I told you so."

XXV

And that *is* the end of the story. Threads of the plot, of course, are much longer than the weave of the cloth. Life goes on.

The home run, once we were out of the core, was clean and easy. I could handle anything, by that time, without breaking into a sweat. I didn't bother to make a landfall —just keep plugging on for fifty-some hours, on shots and intravenous feeding. Medically, it wasn't too good for me, but no matter how long the outward-bound journey takes, the homeward bounder always grates on my nerves so that I can't wait to be rid of it.

Once we were down on Hallsthammer, I began missing events because I needed so much sleep in order to catch up.

Rothgar collected his pay and lit out for somewhere else. He'd had a bellyful.

DelArco successfully evaded Charlot's probing about what had gone wrong with his precious monitor. I don't think the old man ever believed our story, but he could never pick holes in it, and it held up. But the old bastard still held the whip hand, of course. I was still the pawn in his game. There'd be other jobs. He'd have his pound of flesh whether he drained me of blood or not.

A few months later, a Khormon sought me out to tell me that there was a new nova out beyond the Halcyon rim. I calculate that the light should reach Khor in about a hundred and twenty years. By then, it will be just another star in their sky. And a transient one at that.